You Want to Die, Johnny?

by Gavin Black

"Gavin Black doesn't just develop a pressure plot in suspense, he adds uninfected wit, character, charm, and sharp knowledge of the Far East to make rereading as keen as the first race-through."   —*Book Week*

"... has the distinct flavor of the Far East and there is plenty of action."   —*Best Sellers*

GAVIN BLACK

You Want to Die, Johnny?

PERENNIAL LIBRARY
Harper & Row, Publishers
New York, Hagerstown, San Francisco, London

A hardcover edition of this book was originally published by Harper and Row
Publishers, Inc.

First PERENNIAL LIBRARY edition published 1979.

ISBN: 0-06-080472-6

79 80 81 82 83 10 9 8 7 6 5 4 3 2 1

To Helen and T. G. Muir

ONE

THE big Boeing swung around into the arrival bay in front of the Singapore airport buildings. With me beyond the crowd barrier were ten reporters and half a dozen photographers, as well as the ground crew. The plane blustered at us, jet pitch altering, trundling on a collision course with a lot of expensive glass. It turned again just in time, snarling in the hot, still air, then suddenly shut up, becoming less monstrous, somehow settling, as though awfully tired from that long flight across the Pacific.

They got the steps up to the first-class door quickly and the V.I.P.'s came bouncing down one by one with an executive keenness for a new challenge waiting. One of them was an ex-president of the local Chamber of Commerce who didn't like me and had said publicly at the Tanglin Club that the best news of his year was my decision to buy a house two hundred miles to the north in Kuala Lumpur. His sharp eyes picked me out and tightened lips spat out their little message. He waggled a briefcase full of dollar contracts, but not at me, and led the rush toward the exit gates.

Most of the tourist crowd had cleared the plane, too, by the time Sir John Harpen, K.C.M.G., appeared at the front gangway with his daughter. John looked like a tropic resident who has had to go to America in a hurry during the winter, finding that his one heavier suit has grown just a shade too small, binding him all the time he was away. I moved up behind the clump of men with notebooks and those others already lifting cameras.

John turned and said something to his daughter, who didn't seem too responsive. At eighteen Lil was a lush little piece, with puppy fat turning sexy. Her breasts pointed out at the world through a check shirt and her thighs seemed about to rupture tight blue jeans. She had brown hair allowed down to her shoulders and covering her eyebrows. The last time I had seen Lil she had tucked a hand into mine like a girl child who is going to trust men no matter what happens. It's an approach which doesn't always pay off.

John came first, leading the attack, broad-shouldered, glowering, wanting to use his fists but remembering he was a top-level colonial servant. Lil didn't shelter behind that back; she took her own time, and when the camera-clicking and the shouting began, didn't appear to notice at all. She looked like that rare thing, a film star who has made enough money not to give a damn if she gets a poor press. The girl had personality which triumphed over tender years. They had thought so in the States, too.

I wondered how bad the questions would get and they got pretty bad. John began to look all father and an angry one.

"Let us through there! Out of the way!"

I didn't know whether he had seen me or not, but I signaled the car which had been waiting tucked in behind a shed. It moved out onto the runway. Well down on this, away from the buildings, a little four-seater plane was also doing a preliminary trundle, the noise of its twin engines audible above voices.

"Miss Harpen! After what's happened have you any plans to marry Boots Kinsley?"

Lil was by then two thirds of the way down the gangway stairs. She paused on them, put both hands on the shiny, hot metal rail, leaned forward slightly and spat in the reporter's face.

She could have been waiting for this opportunity. Her target

[2]

was a European in a crowd of Chinese who were pleased to laugh at him.

The reporter used his handkerchief and John saw this, but he didn't turn, continuing down the last two steps, demanding passage, dignity remaining though his face was suddenly wet with sweat.

The car came up behind me and I opened the rear door.

"Lil!" John called out.

She was oozing through reporters, still not seeing them, and not hearing them, either. She kept her head down for the cameras, a little mime of modesty which somehow gave the feeling of a hissing bomb that could go off at any moment. The reporters must have felt this, too, for they let her into the car. The attack was turned on the father.

"What are your immediate plans, Sir John?"

"I'm returning to Bintan. To do my job."

"Even after what's happened?"

That stung him.

"Certainly! Now will you please leave us alone? I have nothing to say. Neither does my daughter."

I shut the back door and got in with the driver. The reporters tumbled to the fact that we were making for that small plane and most of them went streaking off for telephones in the airport buildings.

I turned my head.

"Your bags are coming on the mail plane."

"Thanks," he said.

His hands were fists on his knees. He was staring at them. He was a man I had always liked and I felt for him then the kind of compassion which makes you ashamed.

It took half a minute to reach the small plane. Two of the reporters tried to catch us on foot, but we did a quick transit from car to cabin. The pilot slammed the door, revved the engines, and the little job went whizzing down the runway to wait for clearance from control. I was in the front seat, with John and Lil behind.

"They recognized me all right," I said. "That means phone calls to Kuala Lumpur. But I've arranged that we come down at Bahau and drive from there."

"Thanks," John said. It seemed to be all he could say.

I was conscious of Lil looking at me. She had on that hideous ashcan make-up, lips powdered over what appeared to be a blue base, everything else dead-white except eyes, which were Nefertiti-black and aped ancient Egypt. If she was feeling hot no moisture had begun to seep through the coating on her face.

The pilot got clearance. We taxied down a main runway and took the air with that feeling of sodden heaviness at the moment of lift which is the norm with small planes in the tropics. Then a heat thermal lifted us and while we banked I could see reporters at the terminal buildings still out in front of the barrier, gazing up. The getaway had been neat enough, but the attack would be resumed.

The last time I had seen John was a year and a half earlier, over in his Bintan residency. Lil had been at school in England then, at one of those institutions designed to compensate fathers for not having a son, in that the fees are as high as Eton's. You put your girl's name down on the day she is born in the same way, too, and in due course hand her over to a polished dragon who almost guarantees to turn out a lady or your money back. However, they're promising less these days because such odd things happen. Lil was one of them.

I read all about it one morning at breakfast. The daughter of Bintan's top colonial servant had hit American headlines with something of a wham, to my total surprise on tour there with a guitar quartet called the Bangers who had invaded the States from London's East End. Lil didn't seem to be along in any professional capacity, just a companion for the leader, Boots Kinsley. And where Boots went she went, fight-

[4]

ing by his side the mobs of fans. A girl in as close attendance as that might have been expected to cut down Boots' popularity rating but it hadn't. Apparently millions of female teenagers saw in Lil a projection of themselves and at astonishing speed a cult had built up around her, involving total acceptance of an ex-schoolgirl's clothes, manners, accent and philosophy of life. The great big climax to all this had come at a news conference in Los Angeles where Lil had said to television cameras on a cross-country hookup: "Boots and I think God is a drag."

From American adults came a howling noise then which might have been healthier if it had been papas caning their young, with mamas wringing their hands in the background, but it was still a loud protest. I got a phone call from across the South China Sea. John, not very coherent, was on his way to the States. Would I help him? I would, and this was it. A British Resident of an oil Sultanate had then arrived in California where he gave a British guitar player a black eye and flew out again with his daughter.

Over Johore it got a bit bumpy and we had to strap ourselves in. The Chinese pilot looked bored, like most air taxi drivers, his face polished indifference. If he knew who his passengers were, he didn't care. We could have talked, I suppose, even over engine noise, but didn't.

The sick feeling for John persisted. He was my good friend and he was also one of the best men at his job I've known. Oil-rich Bintan had stayed out of the Federation of Malaysia and was still a British protectorate because of this, with a Crown Resident whose role was that of an advisor to the Sultan, Abdul el Badas.

El Badas, whose family have been the hereditary rulers for only a hundred years, loves the money oil is earning him and appears to care not one damn about the people he rules. The Resident has the thankless task of trying, gently, to bring a modern note into a feudal tyranny which in its present form is just an invitation to trouble set out on a gold-plated salver.

John has no power to tell the Sultan what to do. Colonial administration, where it still survives, has to be very cautious; all the United Nations are watching. Officially Bintan is in a transitional phase toward independence, whatever that may mean, and there is a freedom party, headed by the ruler's youngest brother, which has a membership of fourteen, all of them in some way on the oil company's revenue pipeline and wanting an increased flow into their pockets.

John was only thirty when he was appointed Resident, for in those days the main oil area hadn't been exploited and Bintan was just a little blob on the map of Borneo. He had held the position for twelve years, earning a Knighthood he deserved in the process. The fact that there is a modern hospital, any roads at all, and an elementary school system of sorts is entirely due to John's bringing what pressures he could on a collection of ex-Dyak pirates who have assumed the mantle of royalty and gone soft with good living.

Since his wife's early death John has had two loves in his life, Lil and Bintan—I think in that order, though I'm not sure. He did his best for Lil. He flew home to see her whenever he could and had her out on school holidays. When this wasn't possible she was nurtured by loving aunts. He gave her far too much money far too young, which was the natural error of a doting widower, but she seemed to be growing up just a nice kid with no hint at all of the teen-age female Frankenstein who was suddenly to emerge.

I knew that now, and probably all the way to America, and even while he was punching Boots on the nose, and all the way back again, John was blaming himself for what had happened, thinking he was a father who had put his job first and his daughter second.

This just wasn't true and I wanted to tell him so in that little bouncing plane, to bring him the comfort, if it is one, of pointing out that he was up against a phenomenon of our

[6]

time, the teen-age explosion into often vicious prominence which is something resistant to most kinds of parental care. The new Lil wasn't a product of neglect at all; she was part of the big shout of contemporary juvenile protest against a world about which it knows damn all. God and everyone over twenty-one are a drag to a generation suddenly come to puberty at unpleasant speed. It is a kind of vast, world-wide genetic aberration with singularly nasty social consequences, these mainly the result of an unscrupulous adult exploitation of the situation to make a fast buck. And plenty old enough to know better have gone along with the tide, in apparent terror of the label of square. No wonder the kids have got big-headed.

There were a lot of things I could have told John in that plane and, as though she sensed it, Lil sat there staring at my short-back-and-sides haircut. I didn't turn to confirm that she was doing this, I just knew. The girl was giving out strong, subtelepathic emanations.

Bahau only offers a very elementary landing strip with secondary jungle on one side and rubber trees on the other, a length of tarmac left over from World War II and pretty bumpy from sun blisters. The pilot was chewing gum to keep himself relaxed and looked a bit too relaxed to me, but then they always do. I thought his approach speed was too high and the flaps didn't go down until half a minute after I'd have dropped them. A wheel touched one of the tarmac boils and the little plane reared up from that like a jumpy horse. The pilot leveled out and went down again, about fifteen miles above landing speed, keeping a reserve in case he had to gun the engines for a quick climb out. Then he decided to stay down and we began to make a teeth-jarring progress too fast over potholes. My stomach wasn't happy even before the loud bang under us.

What happened then was quick. The wing tip on my side

almost touched. The tail came up. I heard the crack of a prop going and saw a piece of it coming at me. I ducked. Safety glass shattered. The pilot gave a loud, thin shriek but cut the engines. For seconds it was like being in the stomach of a decapitated chicken going through the ritual last throes. Then the long lalang grass and a deep ditch received us. We went down nose first with the sound of loosened metal settling, suspended by safety belts, and with the pilot squawking a protest.

It was fire I thought of, spilled fuel and hot engines. If that was going to happen it would be a sudden whoosh, no time to get out of belts. I took a deep breath and began struggling with my buckle.

"Close," John said, from behind and above.

"How's Lil?"

"All right."

It was her father again. She didn't speak for herself in the company of squares, even under stress conditions.

"You're bleeding," John said.

So was the pilot. Something had fallen on him, and there was an ooze from just above a clipped hairline. He started to thrash about, frenzied, and got his feet up on the control panel. I did the same. The buckle clicked open.

Dial glass crunched under one foot as I kicked with the other at the door by my side. This fell off, dropping about six feet to the bottom of the irrigation ditch. The pilot wailed again. Maybe he was concerned with salvage but for my part I was glad to have all that fresh air coming in. The smell of gasoline fumes eased off at once.

I put the pilot through the hole first. He had a long jump and didn't like it, teetering on the edge, squatting like a matron who knows the water is going to be cold. I kicked him and he left us.

Lil came next, handed down by her father who still hung up in the back of the cabin. Briefly the girl was in my arms, a solid piece of adolescence, but she jumped without the kick.

[8]

John and I didn't stand on ceremony, the engines would still be hot and the fuel would still be spreading.

From the bottom of the ditch there seemed to be a lot of scrap metal above us. No one was going to be able to patch this job together again. The pilot was weeping, seeing that. People have strange loves.

There was a rustling in the long grass and I saw Ohashi peering down through it. He is my aide and a lot of other things, all teeth when he smiles and all horizontal lines under spectacles in a broad flat face when he doesn't. He was carrying a fire extinguisher.

"You okay?" Ohashi shouted.

"Fine. Did you bring the car?"

"Yes, here."

We climbed the bank, through the sword grass—that is, all of us except the pilot. He was in mourning in an old culvert.

The Mercedes was sitting there. I hadn't heard it drive up, but then one didn't. It is a 300 SL with a fuel injection engine. Until I bought my new house in Kuala Lumpur that car was my only real home.

Ohashi opened a back door and Lil climbed in without looking at anyone. Plane wrecks didn't affect her, or it didn't show under that dead-white make-up. She had a smudge on one cheek but that was all. John was quite unbattered. What blood I was producing didn't seem deep-rooted in pain and a handkerchief was all I needed to get tidy again.

"We'd better get the pilot up here," I said. "You get in with Lil, John."

Ohashi shut the door on him, then turned to me. His voice was soft.

"Mr. Harris, you are shot!"

"I'm what?"

"No, not you in body. Plane."

"Come again?"

"I hear it. Three shots. An airplane tire, I think."

[9]

"You're sure you didn't just hear our blowout?"

"No. Shots first. Through engine sound. Quite clear."

Ohashi's eyesight was far from 20-20 but nature had compensated with his ears.

"Where from?"

"I think that woods."

He was pointing toward the rubber plantation. John was looking at us, and began to turn down a window. I heard something, a grating noise a good way off in the rubber, gears engaged. There was a car under those trees, moving off. Whoever was in it had waited in order to take back a full report.

"Get in," I said to Ohashi.

"Pilot?"

"Leave him. He's not hurt."

I ran around to the driver's door.

"What's this?" John asked.

"Party, it looks like. Seems we were shot down."

"How?"

"We can analyze things later."

The Merc was much smoother on that rotten tarmac than the plane had been, but it still didn't like it much. Quite a test of suspension. I pushed through the gears thinking about an irrigation ditch on the other side of the field. It was certainly there, you don't build strips without them in the tropics, but I could see moldering huts which had been built back into the rubber, put there for cover from yesterday's air attacks. Those huts had once had some kind of bridge to them over the ditch and it might still be standing.

It was, marked by a track to it obviously used by rubber-tapping Tamils going to work. I could just see the planks. I took a wild gamble and pushed the car at them, over grass sprouting from cracked asphalt, then with a spurt of speed out onto the kind of wooden structure which rots away quickly in a hot climate, often only continuing to stand as a shell hollowed out by ants.

We bumped and bumped again. I jammed down the accelerator and the Merc practically became airborne, just in time. In my mirror I saw a plank swing up, then the rest crumpling away, with dust, but bite stayed in our driving wheels. I also saw in those seconds Lil there in the back, sitting bolt upright on seats that nearly forced you to relax. On the dead-white face of a young mummy was a half smile.

Rubber is planted in neat symmetry, row after row of what look like park trees, each slowly bleeding white sap into suspended cups. There are laterite access roads patterned through an estate and almost always the area between the trees, though thick with leaf mold, is kept clear of any other growth. I had never driven a car down a rubber aisle before, but I began to do it, and we skidded, with the feel of being on soft snow. Even with the risk of hidden stumps speed had to be kept up for traction and I only went down one gear. We hit sixty on wet leaves, the kind of conditions hard to reproduce in any factory test. The Merc whined at me sometimes and I couldn't blame it.

I saw the other car, just a flick of it between tree trunks, running at right angles on what must be an estate road. It was about a quarter of a mile away and going fast. I saw it again, a jeep utility truck with the back portion canvased-over. However fast it went I knew that on a highway I could drive circles around that thing and light a cigarette doing it. But meantime it would be so easy never to reach the kind of surface a motorcar is made to run on.

Oddly enough I saw a cobra over in the next aisle, and very briefly, but it was sitting up on its tail, outraged, as it had reason to be. The Tamils had better watch out tomorrow during working hours. Any understanding they had reached with snakes had been violated.

There was a barrier between us and the red laterite road, a mound of earth I saw I couldn't take head-on.

"Get out," I said to Ohashi. "Take the car mats with you.

I'll slow down but I can't stop. I want those mats under wheels when I take that bank. I'll do it at an angle. Get it?"

"Yes."

John passed over the rear mat. Ohashi yanked the front one from under my feet. He made a bundle of them both, clutching it to him, and rolled out of his door like a paratrooper going down a few thousand. The leaves were a nice cushion and I could see him up again and running behind us. We were losing traction badly. He had to give me the boost of one mat even before I began to maneuver for an oblique approach to the bank. The rear wheels started a really close fight with leaves and we danced from this, a horrible slack swinging from side to side.

John jumped out, too, with a car rug. I could see now that there wasn't a ditch along the road, which was something.

"I'll clear leaves off the crest here," John shouted. "That'll get you over."

It did. We thumped down from a height onto laterite ridges. John and Ohashi fell into their seats again. The engine said thanks for a surface it could use and took us down red clay ruts at seventy miles an hour, the springs ironing out the corrugations. I got up to seventy-eight at one point where there was a straight. Ahead a truck passing indicated the highway. It was my guess that the jeep would be going south on that road toward Singapore.

Nearly all the main roads in Malaya are good, graded, well-surfaced and fast. Like the Romans the British left this evidence of their skills behind them. The Merc hit a hundred without wind noise, the air conditioning functioning smoothly. Ohashi shoved a lit cigarette into my mouth, as a little prize. We passed an upcoming, rattling bus which almost seemed to be motionless. Lil was still sitting forward, still smiling. Action seemed to have restored John. He looked almost refreshed, the tightness gone from his face.

"What do we do when we catch them?" he asked.

[12]

"See what they do first."

We saw that soon enough. A bend later the jeep was two hundred yards ahead of us, flapping, jolting canvas. I didn't notice the gun poking out the back until a bullet came through our windscreen and went out the rear window, between father and daughter. The glass in front of Ohashi was a mist of little cracks but there were clear patches I could see through on my side, just enough. I began to push the car about on a road empty of upcoming traffic, from side to side. My Japanese aide didn't ask questions, he reached under the facia and glove compartment to a little concealed box we had fitted, bringing out a Webley. He turned down the window beside him and we heard a roaring like the soundtrack switched on.

"I'll pass him on the bridge," I said. "He has to turn in for it and that'll throw out the gunner's aim. Get the inside front tire as we go by."

"Sure," Ohashi said.

He was nearsighted, but within his vision range, and with his specs on, could plug anything. Learning how to was a little hobby I'd taught him, the boy a willing pupil. About half the Japanese who once swept down through Southeast Asia with their guns had been wearing specs, too.

I put the Merc up to a hundred and ten. We swallowed the road to the jeep, which was all out about eighty, and bouncing. The driver could sideswipe us there on the bridge if I gave him time to think about it, but I didn't mean to. If we were shot at again no hits were scored. Passing the jeep I slowed and Ohashi leaned out of the window. The Webley made a positively gentlemanly noise twice. Then I accelerated.

What happened showed in my mirror. The jeep went from its own side straight across the road, up an incline, into a vast hardwood tree and then disappeared down a slope, taking a lot of secondary jungle with it.

When we got out of the Merc the monkeys were screaming

but nothing else. From the scarred hardwood we looked down. The jeep hadn't dropped far, but its wheels were in the air.

"You'd better stay here with Lil," I said to John.

A soft-top jeep is a great car for heavy going, except when it rolls over with people inside. All that weight of chassis is rough on human bones. There had been three Chinese in this one, traveling away from us fast, and none of them were ever going to answer questions again.

There were three rifles in the wreckage, all of Czechoslovak make, one with a telescopic sight, expensive pieces.

"The license plates are real," I said.

"So jeep is stolen?"

"Certain. Just as certain as the police will never identify these men. I think you'd better turn the car and we'll go home."

"How do we explain windscreen?"

"A stone hit us."

"Rear window, too?"

"We can get a replacement for that locally. When we get back smash every bit of glass out of it. Before you take the car to our garage. They won't chat to the police. Not with what we pay them. And it'll be dark in twenty minutes. I'll go a back way into K. L. We'll take the guns. Better not to have the police find them."

"We leave men here?"

"Yes. I hate assassins."

The monkey twittering subsided while Ohashi was away turning the car on another stretch of road. The jungle settled back to norm except for one irritated old gibbon who went into a boring sermon about the decadence of the age which even had Lil turning her head to look up. There's something a shade unnerving about monkey sermons until you're heard a lot of them.

We were in the light flare before a dropped dark, an orange-and-red glow above the hardwoods flanking both sides of the highway. I heard the hum of tires a long way off, from the wrong direction for the Merc, and John and Lil made no protest about withdrawing into a screen of growth while the car passed. We waited for the sound of brakes which meant the driver had spotted scrape marks across the road, and jungle damage, but he didn't stop, if anything went a little faster. Some years ago a tradition grew up in this country of not loitering on roads at dusk, or any other time, which hasn't really quite broken down yet. There aren't any Red ambushes these days, but one remembers.

The Merc slid up and then with a load of guns and us slid away again. It was very soon dark and we ceased to be conspicuous as having been in the wars. I knew back roads through all of the towns ahead.

"When are you going to stop at a police station to make your report?" John asked.

"I'm not going to."

"I see."

There was a judicial, suspended silence from the back seat.

"The police couldn't do anything," I said. "And think of the publicity for you."

"I have been thinking about it. Don't use me as an excuse for doing exactly what you meant to do anyway."

I laughed. "Were the plane wreckers after you or me or both?"

"You, I should think," John said.

"I wonder? These days I'm totally respectable. I even moved north from Singapore to help me build up the new image."

"Like a Mafia boss shifting to a garden suburb?"

"Unkind. The facts are that I don't think anyone is gunning for the new worthy citizen. It would be easy enough to get me without shooting down a plane. I walk to the office most mornings, totally unarmed."

Ohashi laughed then. The Japanese use laughter to cover uneasiness.

[15]

I found the boy in Tokyo. I am his elder brother and expect to be engaged as go-between when he makes up his mind it is time to marry some local girl. One way of dealing with the terrible industry of the Japanese is to harness a little of it on your side. What I pay him would have already made him a mildly rich man even in booming Yedo, and he knows it. He also knows he's worth every penny.

People say that the Japanese are the most pragmatic people on earth, with no souls. It's a miscalculation. They are terrible realists, but with this conditioned by a potential in emotional loyalty that verges on the sentimental. Loyalty is their real motivation as a race, and there are worse things. You can hitch loyalty onto a lot of objects, good or bad, and it produces an effectiveness which is lethal to competition. It wouldn't astonish me to know for certain that if Harris and Company went into liquidation Ohashi would commit honorable cut belly on a white sheet, facing toward the Imperial Palace, or perhaps toward my new head office. But he'd have put up one hell of a fight first to save the business.

John stayed silent and probably thoughtful. He was in the position of being hi-jacked away from Colonial Service first principles which are always to do things through the proper channels. However, I knew perfectly well that over in Bintan the Resident had at times adopted tactics which would have scandalized Whitehall if word had got home. I hoped he was going to allow me the same latitude in Malaya as he permitted himself in his own territory though, of course, I wasn't a British Resident.

"Isn't our pilot going to talk?" he asked suddenly. "He must have seen our car belting off into the rubber. Which was a curious way to leave the airstrip."

"I don't think he did see us. He was down in that ditch worrying. A lot of people simply can't bring themselves to believe in insurance."

"There could be a bullet hole in the plane."

[16]

"Ohashi is sure they were shooting at the tires. The pilot doesn't know about the shooting at all. And who is going to look for anything in that heap of junk if we don't talk? There's no mystery about a crack-up on a strip like that."

"Only about three dead men found in a jeep."

"Seven miles away. A nasty road accident of the kind that happens all the time. No guns found, no questions asked. Where's the tie-up with us?"

"We are."

"Only one bus saw us. The Mercedes is a popular car in Malaya. And the owners tend to drive fast. There's not much point in having one if you don't."

"Paul, why do you want to cover this up?"

"To give us time to assess things. Particularly if someone wants you dead."

TWO

AFTER some time John said: "You have a melodramatic mind."

"From my patterns. And it is also a fact that the Far East is high melodrama these days. Every inch of it."

"No one wants to kill me."

"How do you know?"

"Possibly because I can't see myself as an effective threat to anything."

"Travel given you perspective?"

"The moment I leave Bintan I get complete perspective. On what I'm doing and what I have done. You could draw a line under it and put zero."

"Not for my money."

"For the facts of our time. My job is something left over from the first half of the twentieth century. A British Resident is a dodo bird. One day they'll have a museum for colonial relics and in it will be a stuffed Resident in full regalia."

Lil laughed. The effect of that sound was curious, it seemed to come from somewhere a long way beyond us, outside, and a comment. Her laugh was the kind of cruelty some believe in permitting the young because of their innocence of real, continuing pain. But I wondered then if John had ever used a whippy cane on his daughter's behind. My father believed in the backside of a hairbrush at regular intervals for his sons. It's an effective instrument, too. It turned us into sound businessmen, who contrived to be something a little more than management executives in someone else's corporation. And if my father had been given daughters I doubt if he would have altered his disciplinary techniques for the weaker sex.

Ahead of us was the glow of massed light on low clouds. Kuala Lumpur has seen a lot of mushroom growth recently as the capital of Malaysia but it still remains a small town at heart, inhabited by a population who don't really believe in contemporary pressures at all, whatever act they put on about them. It is a city of huge trees left over from jungle, of shade from sun, colonnaded buildings in the old colonial style still dominant in spite of modern blocks, and a feel of hills present in the town itself, with mountains available just behind. At considerable cost and in competition with a development company I bought my own little hill overlooking the old city. I'm ten minutes' drive from the business center, up a twisting road through suburbs and suddenly through a gate into a private jungle with one spiral approach to the heights. It is nice tame jungle, drained with concrete culverts, and no place for mosquitoes to breed at all.

The house is really an old planter's bungalow stuck down sixty years ago within the city limits. It is all verandas beyond high, cool rooms, using as much ground as it likes and still leaving plenty of space over for wide lawns ending in bougainvillaea and hibiscus hedges. The place is totally uneconomic to run and needs a staff of five—including the gardener—which has been a heavy drain on company profits after tax, but I think worth it. I can still ring up from the Selangor Club that I'm bringing eight people home to dinner in twenty minutes and my cook just likes it. There's no Florida millionaire who can do better than that.

The place looked very pretty when we reached it, all lit up, even the verandas, these dripping with orchids the gardener hangs about the place because they're the easiest thing to grow. Lil got out of the car and just stood there looking like the holder of a world air ticket who has arrived at Agra to see the Taj Mahal by moonlight but is really wondering whether the plumbing is going to be as bad as it was at the last stopover.

I told Ohashi to get the car down quickly to our under- standing garage and then followed John and his daughter up the steps. Lil climbed them without looking at anything, a lot of buttock under travel-creased covering. She didn't look at my number one boy, either. He looked at her.

"If you'd like to shower before drinks," I said, "Chow will show you to your rooms. I'll have whisky waiting."

"I take mine with Coke," Lil announced.

"You'll get the Coke."

Nefertiti eyes said things. It didn't worry me. Lil went off with Chow, but John stayed. We went under one of those ceiling fans I'd kept because I like them. It had to be oiled twice a week or it creaked. It was creaking now. I poured at a table.

I was thinking about what being a parent can involve, the expenditure of means and spirit to a time like this, to blank defeat and a kind of terror beyond. John had sweated all his active life, and against the hard obstacle of a continuing in- difference, to get some brown kids behind desks in schools for a little learning, to get others into beds in a decent hos- pital for a bit more of life instead of the easy death of the East. No one I knew would have taken John's living as a present, for all the big Residency and the moments of pomp, when he wore a sword. He had somehow kept the enthusiasm of a young man for the impossible, knowing that time and circumstances weren't running his way as he tried to bring it about. Little Bintan wasn't a good country with John in it, but it would be hell without him.

One day, when all the yahoo about colonialism has died down and real perspective is available, it will be seen just how many there were like John in the service, with a strange, almost unbearable task as the center duty for which they ex-

[20]

isted. Not popular as a class in retrospect now, even comic in our time, men who lived by rules that have been blown up, but who nonetheless served and who used the power given them in that service. And they were vulnerable in their personal lives because of concentration and absorption, experience to a very large degree limited by massive responsibility, leaving them in the little island of their isolation where they had made a kind of peace that wasn't to last. John saw himself as one of yesterday's men, a survivor, and the hell of it was that it was the truth.

He took his glass.

"Well, Paul, you've been observing my daughter. What's your summing up?"

"I don't have one."

"It isn't obligatory in your case. Unfortunately it is in mine. I don't know what the hell I'm going to do now."

"Is Bintan the place for her?"

"It's where I live."

He looked down at the toecaps of his shoes.

"This is an old problem which is nearly extinct, too. What the Colonial Administrator does about family. Especially the widower. Though, of course, firm rules were laid down, that we must send them home to be turned into strangers. I got the stranger all right."

"Your sisters had no real control of Lil?"

"My sisters have no children of their own. They both live in the country. What's happening in London reaches Dorset and Cumberland as distant echoes. Just about as distant as the echoes around in Bintan. Lil was in London."

"And you let her go to drama school?"

"I wanted her to be happy."

"Has she any talent?"

"A flair for personal publicity at any rate." He smiled. "Isn't that what an actress needs more than anything these days?"

"Have you any idea how she met the guitar player?"

"I should think at a party. Though she hasn't told me. We haven't been exchanging many confidences. All I know is that a great deal has happened to Lil in a year, and I can only guess at part of it. Incidentally, what's to stop her just walking out of here? She might."

"Three Sikhs."

"You mean you have a guard around your house?"

"Yes. For that occasion. Lil won't go anywhere until you've had a chance to sort things out."

"You do go to trouble for your friends." He put down the glass. "Now that bath, I think. Thank you, Paul."

It was a silent dinner, by candlelight, all the bourgeois trappings I'd gone in for with a new house, but no real pretense at a social performance at all. Lil would have enjoyed boycotting this so it seemed a good idea not to offer it. She ate well, the puppy fat tissues still remaining demanded sustenance on a large scale.

I hated the sudden new tensions in my home. It had been without these, artificial perhaps, a place to live which was probably a device for escape, and very nice, too. Even my servants had been carefully chosen for the lack of temperament which so often goes hand in hand with inefficiency, but I enjoyed the sound of somewhat idiot laughter echoing from the kitchen.

It had been all right up on my hill until today. Now I watched Chow going around the table with a slightly puzzled look on his face, like a dog who knows that all is not joy with master, wishing he could help, but only able to wag a tail and look hopeful. It was something. A great many of us have been encouraged by a good dog's hope.

Lil went to bed right after the meal, or at least she said she was going to bed. She thawed enough to bid us goodnight and express her intention, which was a surprising return to graciousness, maybe the result of two helpings of pudding. John

[22]

and I then moved out onto the veranda beyond the living room and I doused the lights, leaving us in a glow from behind for our brandy and Manila cheroots. After a little I went in and switched on the record player, Monteverdi, and the cool, thin boys' voices came out into the motionless tropic air. It's the kind of music for a hot country—intellectuals like Brahms somehow seeming to increase the humidity. The most we can take in comfort is the ultimate in voice orchestration.

After a time we talked, but not about Lil. John told me about recent developments in Bintan, and it was really the picture as before, the place a shambles. Oil, he said, is one of the major disruptive factors of our time in the place where it is located. Inevitably, by its exploitable presence, it creates a situation so far from any workable norm that all existing values are destroyed and a kind of lunatic chaos results. The terrible benevolence of the oil companies, real enough in its way, is still destructive, and usually it is discovered in areas where the life patterns are primitive and totally vulnerable. Bintan might just have been waiting for this great discovery, with its tribal rulers who had been happily engaged in slitting each other's throats suddenly inflated into international importance because of a slime lying under the soil.

The phone rang in the hall and I went to it.

Something about the voice over the wire made me chary at once. It was British, but incredibly lah-di-dah, like a Cockney putting on the dog and not making a very good job of it. The voice asked for Lil.

"Who is this speaking?"

"A friend of hers, old boy."

"Who the hell are you?"

"Does it really matter? Miss Harpen isn't under restraint or anything, is she?"

"I don't know what you mean by that, but if you expect me to answer questions you'll tell me your name."

"It wouldn't ring any bells."

[23]

"If you're a reporter this is a pretty poor dodge to get news. Miss Harpen is resting. Put that in your paper."

"I don't have a paper."

"Lucky for the press," I said, and hung up.

Lil was leaning against an arch watching me.

"I'm not, as it happens, resting," she said. "And I like to take my own calls. There isn't a phone in my room."

"My guests don't usually mind a little walk."

"Who was it?"

"I don't know. But I didn't like the sound of him."

"You wouldn't . . . of my friends."

"Agreed, dear."

She took a step forward.

"If you think you can try the rough stuff with me, guess again."

"Someone should have started long ago."

"Who the hell are you anyway?"

"A friend of your father's. You used to call me Uncle. Remember?"

"I was a fool kid then."

"It's something from which we all recover. Why don't you go to bed? You must be tired."

"I'm not, as it happens. And if anyone rings me, I want to speak to them."

Lil swung around. She was still wearing slacks but had changed her shirt; the luggage had arrived. A dress would probably have been too much to expect.

John came out from the living room.

"What's all this?"

Lil jerked her head around. "Ask him."

Then she went away.

"Someone rang up for Lil. I think it was long distance from Singapore. Would she have friends there?"

"A few. She used to fly out with a girl called Wilson."

"This was a man who didn't give his name. From a paper

probably. The evening ones may have been playing up your arrival."

"I see. Well, we can do without any more statements to the press."

Out on the veranda again I asked John if he was worried about the London reaction to what had happened.

"Yes, I suppose I am, up to a point. The Colonial Office doesn't like scandals involving its faithful servants."

"This isn't a scandal, it's daughter trouble. There are plenty of senior officials in bowler hats commuting every night down into Kent who don't know what they're going to find when they get home with their own daughters. Every damn one of them knows in his heart that what's happened to you could easily happen to him."

"I don't think I can really go along with that, Paul."

"All right. But take no action from your end. Wait for them to make the first move. You'll find they won't. This will blow over."

He reached for the brandy bottle.

"Lil slept with that fellow, all the way across America. She told me that much in a hotel bedroom in Los Angeles."

"And you can't get past that in your thinking? Virginity in our time doesn't have the high market value it used to. Is she pregnant?"

"She says not."

"That's something. John, when did you first hear about all this? The story was splashed in our papers three days before you phoned me."

"I know. I'd been over our border into Sarawak, having a look at things up there. We hear talk of Indonesian infiltration through to us. I'd been away for three weeks, no mail, and I didn't even know Lil was in America. When I got back Ursula Gissing phoned. You remember her?"

I remembered Ursula, who wouldn't? She was the fiftyish wife of John's number two, an Honorable in her own right who felt that her habitat ought to have been hostess in one of those English country houses from which everything used to be manipulated at political weekends. A husband stationed in Bintan cramped her style but she made the best of her environment. If I had bad news coming the last person I'd want to hear it from would be her.

"She was very kind," John said. The irony in his voice was healthy.

"Does Ursula imagine that her husband would be given your job if you left it?"

"It might just be in her mind. But Charlie wouldn't be made Resident."

"No. And to do Charlie justice I don't think he'd want to be on those terms."

"It's interesting that you're willing to do Charlie justice. So many aren't. They find him a silly little man. I don't."

There could be a good reason for that, of course. Charlie was devoted to John. It was a curious devotion for the Colonial Service, apparently unaffected by professional jealousies. I've noticed that the great ones of the earth—and British Residents—like to have a stooge, not a sycophantic one if they're intelligent, but still a man around who wears a large placard saying he hasn't made it and who is busy sublimating personal failure by an almost worshipful enthusiasm for big brother who is right up there. The fact that big brother in this case was eight years Charlie Gissing's junior didn't alter things. Ursula, as might be expected, took a sweet-sour view of all this. For an Honorable to be a stooge's wife was like being put into one of the lower rungs of Gehenna and held there.

"I'm going to bed," John said, getting up.

"Do you have a sleeping pill?"

"Yes. First thing I got in the States. Goodnight. And thanks again."

What I was going to say got choked.

A sound reached us from what seemed halfway down my

hill, a wailing, steepening in pitch and then going very high indeed.

I jumped over the veranda railing, damaging bougain-villaea, and ran across lawn, with John not far behind me, our feet soundless on grass, then thudding on tarmac. There is an electric standard at the top of the drive where it curves around into a parking place and another light about two hundred yards down a steep drop. Under this second light was a turbaned Sikh struggling with something in trousers which we both saw very soon was Lil.

"Let me go, damn you! Let me . . ."

"Mem, you must not to go out. You must not!"

The Sikh was very unhappy. And he wasn't ready for what Lil did next. She fetched back one foot and kicked him hard on the shins.

"Ach . . . !"

There was a certain fury in that, the rage of a character who has been brought up carefully as a woman-beater, faced by a circumstance which can't be dealt with in any traditional manner.

"Let go of her, Gian Singh!"

"But, Tuan, I am only do my dutee."

"I know. And you were quite right to stop her."

"Tuan, I am sitting so. There. So, she comes so gently down, so gently . . ."

"Smelly beast!"

"Shut up, Lil!" That was John. "And apologize."

"Apologize because I'm attacked by a thug?"

"My night watchman."

"Your jailer, you mean!"

"Lil, apologize."

"No!"

John went over then and did something all the books say you mustn't, clonked his daughter one on the side of her head, and no love pat either. It rocked her back on her heels.

[27]

"Get up to the house and go to bed."

I couldn't know whether Gian Singh still retained any faith in the white races at all, but if there was a vestige of this remaining it was reinforced in that moment. From a Sikh point of view daddy had done the right thing.

"I hate you all!" Lil said from about five paces up the road. "I hate you!"

We bore up under that. In fact it seemed to me that John was bearing up remarkably well generally, as a parent. There might even be a solution ahead.

When I got to bed I couldn't sleep and finally quit air conditioning for the natural warmth out on the veranda. In the glow from the city, which like all Eastern ones never seems to sleep, I could just see the onion domes of the *Tunkup's* new university, a symbol of change but not unwelcome. It was change that the place absorbed and took in its stride, the new pride rarely aggressive, just there. It was a beginning and these have their own vitality, something it is good to be part of, whatever my feelings about the new nation had once been. The reactionary in me was fading, and I knew it. Often, these days, I find myself rooting for the new thing, like a ruddy convert.

I drove myself down to the office the next morning in the Ford Anglia, and coming around the last jungle curve into the main suburban road I saw Gian Singh at the gate arguing with someone who had got out of a parked Austin. I leaned out of the window and said:

"No press."

The young man in spotless white had the adhesive persistence of his calling.

"I wish a statement from His Excellency, the Resident of Bintan."

"You won't get it."

"You speak for the Resident?"

"While he's my guest, yes. No one is allowed up to the house."

"Europeans do not give such orders in the new Malaysia!"

I smiled at the boy.

"I'm a Malaysian subject."

That shook him. I didn't renounce my British citizenship for the economic and social advantages that might result from this step, but I'm always delighted to make use of any advantages that may accrue. Not many European businessmen have done what I did, and the government wish more would. For me it was an act of some faith, a good deal of hope, and not a small measure of charity. I have no bank account in Switzerland. If Malaysia as at present constituted falls it looks as though I'll fall with it, a nasty bump for us all.

"Let's have no trouble," I said sweetly and drove on.

Throwing in your lot with a new country is in some ways a curious sensation. The whole Federation is artificial, as the Indonesians keep shouting in the United Nations, but then most federations were once, and it's something that wears off. There are some who claim, and not without reason, that Malaysia is just a nifty dodge on the part of the British to keep a sphere of influence in former colonial territory, the old gang up to a new trick. As one of the old gang, recently converted, I suppose I'm suspect myself in that I'm not losing money and I have no intention of carrying my new patriotism to any point where this begins to happen. In my own way I help stir the pot of trade out here and I intend to live well as my reward. I believe that capitalism, while not necessarily the end of man, is the most efficient economic system yet evolved and my argument is supported by the highest standard of living in the Far East in this little capitalist country to which I am committed body and to a large degree soul as well.

I love the place. I wake up in the morning for early tea and half a papaya to watch the night screen of mist dissolving over jungle trees, with the mountains of the main spine changing a chilly blue for daytime green. You can smell the jungle in Kuala Lumpur just after dawn, a rich hot essence of it, distilled and yet somehow emphasized by the spreading presence of man.

What a country. There is no season of drought, no withering green leaf fighting the old green, hot, but always with relief coming in one of the sudden Sumatras which rattle the shutters, toss the huge hardwoods, batter with rain for twenty minutes, and then let the sun in again. The sun offers eternal largesse, powerful, hard sometimes, but never truly cruel, and the rivers always run full. In the jungle, with the leeches and the mosquitoes, there is fast tumbling water. All around the peninsula is the sea which holds sharks and a gleaming depth of brightness surfaced over in jade and lapis lazuli. There are twenty-mile beaches of gold sand backed by palms and casuarinas without the blot of a single colored hotel umbrella.

The new offices of Harris and Company are in an old building with a colonnade out front, and to reach them you go through a designed coolness of stone which takes the artificial edge off air conditioning. Ohashi, going into his office, turned and grinned at me.

"Car okay," he said, then shut the door.

Mimi looked flustered. I have hopes for the girl, she is learning slowly, but panic still threatens her, as though she lives in constant terror that at any moment I may decide to sack her. Because of this I'm usually as gentle as a new lover.

She is a big girl, who dresses as though she had changed her mind halfway and then hadn't had time to go through with the altered color scheme. She is fond of red, which ought to go well with black hair and black eyes, but is somehow always put on the wrong part of her body.

"Oh, Mr. Harris! Mr. Russell Menzies in Singapore has been trying to get you all morning. I wasn't sure whether I should ring your home about it or not. So I just told him that

I was expecting you soon, though he seemed a bit impatient at the last call. I hope I did the right thing?"

"Perfectly right, Mimi. Lawyers are always impatient. It's part of their act. Get him for me now, will you?"

Russell sounded surly down there in the big city.

"Hello, playboy. How's your nervous indigestion? Because you may need sedation after what I've got to tell you."

He went on with relish to tell me. A rival airliner from the States had come into Singapore two hours after the one carrying Lil and her father. On it had been a British subject by the name of Boots Kinsley. It appears that in our time no one can sock a guitar player and get away with it.

"This character," Russell said, "checked into his hotel suite and then rang down at once to ask who was the best lawyer in town. I'm immensely flattered that they gave him my name. I was then rung up and told to come over pronto. When I said I didn't come over anywhere pronto under any circumstances, Mr. Kinsley seemed a little surprised; he is used to better service. But he came to see me. It was interesting. He isn't just a guitar player. He has something to give the kids that they haven't had before. A kind of spiritual guidance, I gathered. He's a Messiah in tight pants and the world has needed him for a long time. He's also a limited liability company with remarkably unlimited resources. He is now proposing to sue a British Resident under Malaysian law for assault. I thought you would be interested."

"Yes," I said, not very loud. There was suddenly no mystery about the phone call last night.

"It appears there's nothing to stop him, either. He's of age, just. He can put the expenses of defending his public image against tax. He was on the phone to London about that and has got it all fixed with his accountant. I told the young man that, though it hurt me not to take his money, it would probably be unethical for me to act for him in view of my association with you and one thing and another. I didn't say that, anxious as I am to retire and lead the sweet life, I still don't take cases that stink quite as much as this one does. So I sent him to Chang Fa."

"Oh, no!" I said.

"Oh, yes. He'd have found Chang anyway, in a very little time. Our dear colleague, Mr. Chang, can smell something like this from as far off as California. The action will be brought in a court here. Quite soon, I should imagine. I think you'd better put your house guest in the picture damn quick."

"How did you know John was with me?"

"Menzies hears all, sees all, and gets highly paid for what he is prepared to say as a result. Actually, I added things up after reading the full story of fugitive papa and errant daughter."

"The papers don't say anything about Boots Kinsley. Why?"

"Extraordinarily enough the boy came in incognito, under his real name which is Jimmy. But the press is onto him now. You'll soon be reading all about it."

I told Mimi to put any calls through to my house and went back there at speed. John was sitting out on the lawn with Taro, my Japanese Tosa hound. Taro is a big brindle fighting dog who doesn't usually move into any act of man's best friend. All the servants except Chow are scared of him, though he is polite enough to legitimate staff. The postman is always punctual because we chain Taro up around then. When I have friends for drinks the dog sits in my bedroom, not howling, just muttering about parties. He gave me a tail thump but stayed by John.

"Where's Lil?"

"Sleeping apparently. Chow tells me she had breakfast and curled up again."

John was facing the new day with total composure, like a man who has slept well. I hated to disturb that calm and sat down to do it. He listened without moving and without comment, the ash growing long on his cigarette. Then he said:

"Well. An interesting development. I seem to have underrated the boy."

"How did you rate him?"

"I suppose as someone totally outside the norm. You can't be a world celebrity at twenty-one and be in any kind of norm. It never occurred to me that he would follow us, though, or take any action against me."

"What are you going to do about his action?"

"Certainly not fly off the handle as I did in California. I'm taking Lil back to Bintan. Right away. I'd decided to do that, and for another reason. I've been thinking about the plane crash and that it might be a mistake to rule out any idea that the thing was staged for me. I have enemies."

"In Bintan?"

"Forgive me if I don't react to any leading questions, Paul. Even from you."

"Would you be interested in an idea of mine?"

"Very."

"I've been thinking about Bintan, too. The local Chinese ran the country's economy, didn't they, before oil?"

"In so far as I let them."

"Couldn't they resent changed days and not being able to do it any more?"

"They might and probably do."

"I was interested in a man I met in your house when I was over. Yin Tao."

"Oh, yes?"

"Their big man, isn't he?"

"So what?"

"I found him curiously obstructive. After we met I looked him up when he was in Singapore. I thought I had an attractive proposition, but he absolutely refused to use any Harris and Company junks in his local monopoly of birds' nest export. I offered him better terms than he was getting, much. But he just wasn't dealing with a European-controlled business, even though my crews are mainly Chinese. It seemed to me odd."

"Isn't it the kind of prejudice you meet a good deal?"

"No, not that often. Otherwise my business wouldn't be as healthy as it is. Most *hua-chiao* will ship by the cheapest means offering a good and reliable service, which I do. I told Yin Tao that I could switch half my junks based on Palawan to his trade for as much of the year as he needed. He still wouldn't look at it. It made me wonder if the pro-Red China feeling is particularly strong over in Bintan."

"It's strong everywhere," John said.

And that was true enough. *Hua-chiao*, overseas Chinese, play a decisive role in what is going to happen in Southeast Asia. It's a thought that comes to me when I'm not sleeping at night. And in Bintan, before the miracle of oil, the Sultan had been tied up in debt to the Chinese, their man because of this. The fact that he wasn't their man any longer almost certainly rankled. It's not pleasant to lose power suddenly.

No country has ever yet assimilated its Chinese. Singapore millionaires, who owe their fortunes to a grandfather's emigration, still sit on the fence when it comes to loyalties, carefully refraining from any impiety toward big brother Mao. China's foreign currency problem is partly solved by apparently willing contributions in dollars from characters who ought to hate everything the new regime stands for because, under it, they would be eliminated. In fact only a handful of Malayan Chinese businessmen outside of Formosa are openly hostile to Mao, the rest set off firecrackers in the courtyards of their tropic baroque palaces to celebrate a Chinese atomic bang.

This is true of the directors of a marine engine company in Johore in which I am a partner. I get on perfectly well with these men, but without any illusions. For them Malaysia is a fact of the time, useful to them at the moment, but it has never laid any claim on their hearts. It isn't only the rioting Red students in Singapore who would welcome a greater China in Asia; most of the capitalists have an emotional attachment to the same idea. They see that Mao's China would be lethal to them at the moment, but have vague hopes for the kind of change at home which would permit them to survive at the periphery, with all their carefully acquired creature comforts. And Mao even plays up to this hope with a cute little drama staged in Peking itself, where a handful of carefully selected businessmen are permitted to continue as "capitalists" earning sizable profits.

You can't argue with my partners. They dance away from this, inviting you to a heart-of-palm banquet where the main dish costs two hundred dollars a plate. I know that at least two of them contribute to numbered accounts in that convenient little central European country as regularly as they do to Mao. Experience has taught them to believe in insurance policies.

John stood.

"Lil and I will be on the afternoon plane to Latuan, even if it means a couple of other passengers chucked off to make room. Can I count on Harris and Company getting us to Singapore in time?"

"Yes," I said. "Has Lil seen the papers this morning?"

"No. And she won't see any papers today."

"What if Boots Kinsley decides to visit Bintan?"

He smiled.

"He won't get a landing permit."

It's quite a help with parental problems to be in a position to keep unwanted boy friends out of your country.

"You'll watch out, won't you?" I said.

"I'll watch out. I've done it all my life. And a sudden appearance in Bintan of the Resident ought to put the enemies of light to flight."

"I hope."

"So do I. But if things get too tricky I can always send for the Harris private navy. Do you have a gun on your flagship these days?"

"Not mounted."

"But still the same semipiratical crews?"

"Our approach to Southeast Asia trade isn't always strictly conventional. That's all I'll say."

"It's quite enough. I'll stop wondering about that ramming of an Indonesian patrol boat last month off Pulao Roepat."

"An accident on the high seas," I said. "Collision on a dark night."

"Yes. And your junk with concealed armor plating on its bows came off best."

"You have no evidence of armor plating."

"I don't need it. I still think you're the one who should be looking after your health."

"But I do all the time. This is really a little fortress. Guarded by watchmen and killer dogs."

John looked at the killer dog, who was panting.

"Hm. Nice beast. I keep thinking about getting one."

THREE

THE Boots Kinsley action against Sir John Harpen was mentioned in the Malaysian press but without any subtle hints of exciting installments to follow. John was popular in the country, for his efforts to bring Bintan into the Federation were well-known and, if anyone was, he was their man. Perhaps the local attitude on this matter was made known in London, too, for though I watched the English papers there was no hint in any of them that trouble lay ahead for the Resident. One of the popular dailies ran a feature: "If you were a father would you have socked Boots?" with the writer clearly suggesting that the proper answer was yes. The Bangers were beginning to get a bad press, as though Fleet Street was just a shade tired of them, reporters weary at last of being pushed around in teen-age mobs.

Boots flew off from Singapore to meet his boys in Japan and to three engagements in Tokyo, Yokohama, and Kobe from which it was said that their take-home pay after tax and expenses would be another fifteen thousand pounds for six hours' work. On the steps up to his plane Boots echoed General MacArthur with a statement that he would be back, but this didn't cause any excitement and it was rumored that the A.P. man had stayed in the airport bar drinking whisky, only moving to the windows to wave a swizzle stick as the jet taxied out for takeoff.

I thought everything was quietening down nicely until Russell Menzies rang me up.

"Hello, evacuee," he said. "How's the tempo of life up there with you?"

Russell had not approved of the Harris and Company move north. He hated to be slightly out of the picture, particularly where his own interests were concerned. He also envied me the better air.

"Comfortable," I said.

"Then let me jerk you awake. The Kinsley hearing is set for three weeks from now. Chang took it on, as we both suspected he would. Kinsley thinks his image has been nicked to the amount of thirty thousand quid. How's the Resident of Bintan going to take that?"

"Calmly, I should think."

"Kinsley won't get those damages, he mightn't get any, but the betting down here is that he'll get costs. When Chang has everything set up on that side these should amount to about twenty thousand pounds."

"Nonsense!"

"You don't know Chang. He's fetching out Californian witnesses. This is the star feature of his year. He's due for a bit of a flash in public as a change from private ransom arrangements for local towkays' favorite girl friends. Would it be your guess that Sir John has twenty thousand to lose?"

"I shouldn't think so for a moment. He's a career man. I don't believe there's any family money at all."

"Tsk, tsk," Russell said. "Then he'll have to face penniless retirement in a Brighton boarding house."

"Russell, do you really mean this?"

"Cross me fat heart. It's going to happen."

"Even if you were booked for the defense and we got a Q.C. out from England?"

"I've told you I'm not touching this, on moral grounds. That and the fact that I wouldn't like to be on the losing side against Chang. It's one of the things I've always avoided carefully. You could get Willie Clamp if you wanted."

"Would he be able to stop the rot?"

"No."

"What the hell good are lawyers anyway?"

"Coming from you to me, who's been your wet nurse for so long, that's rude."

"Look, John oughtn't to have to take this, on top of everything else at the moment."

"You've got me weeping down here. If you want to be a boy scout you could pay costs. Your accountants and I might be able to wangle it against tax as a legitimate business expense. There's a great deal of local sympathy for Harpen, and even the revenue boys have hearts, especially if they're tipped off to have them from someone right up there in your nice air-conditioned capital. Get me?"

"Yes. But John wouldn't play. Not for a minute."

"Then he's for the high jump financially. Sympathy he'll get, plenty of it, but Chang will still be able to bleed him. It's a crook lawyer's world, friend, as I'm sadly reminded every time I get my bank statement. If I were you I'd do my duty right away and let Sir John know what he's up against. It's only basic kindness really. Your friend may be one of those characters who thinks that the law is primarily concerned with seeing justice done."

"And isn't it?"

"There are some millions of alimony-paying ex-husbands in the Western world who would give the big horse laugh to that. They know."

I didn't phone John for a day, which was probably wrong. When I did book a call I had to wait two hours to get through and a line was open to the Residency about midnight, the perfect time for bad news. I pushed all the facts over that wire, crowding them at him, and all he said at the end was: "I see." After a deep breath he added:

"You're quite sure about all this?"

"Russell is and he knows."

"Well, I shall have to start mustering my forces, won't I?"

"John, will you remember that those include me?"

"The Harris navy?"

"No, the Harris bank account," I said bluntly.

"That's not on."

"I've never had the chance to call a British Resident a clot, but I'm doing it now. My real friends are few and I value them. Also, there is no little brood of Harrises waiting in the nest squawking for a million-dollar trust fund each so that they'll be able to make their mark in the world."

"There are still plenty of charities and I'm not one."

"John, for God's sake listen to sense! Nothing would give me greater pleasure than an indirect swipe at the Boots Kinsleys of our time."

"Then start buying up record companies and refuse to record them."

"All right, I haven't put this very subtly. I'm not a subtle type. But my reasons for wanting to back you on this are not entirely personal. I think you're a man in a place which needs a man like you at the moment. It's in my business interests to see that you stay there."

"Indeed?" said the British Resident.

"Oh, hell. I'm making a mess of this."

"You are, but I give you full marks for trying. Perhaps I should tell you, even on an open line, that I've just had a summons, from ministerial level, to London. Ostensibly for talks on the Bintan situation. But it is an order. And it could mean that I won't be coming back to my old job."

After a minute I said:

"They wouldn't dare replace you."

"I think they might."

"What about Lil?"

"I'm taking her with me. There's no use keeping her here. It's getting us no place."

"John, would it be any help if I came over?"

"No. You're on Lil's square list, too. Second place. You're not Uncle any more."

"I know that."

"And I'm not Father."

Mimi hadn't been with me long enough to have any previous experience of ushering in the police. There were traces of panic in her voice at the announcement she had to make. Inspector Kang moved deftly past her, waited for her dismissal, then shut the door himself.

"Well, Mr. Harris?"

There was a time when the Inspector had done his best to get me inside a Singapore jail, then changed his mind at the last minute. It's always remained a bond between us. I gave him a cheroot and my best chair. He crossed his legs like a man who has got on well enough not to have to bother about the creases. He was, as always, immensely dapper in uniform, a handsome man really, in a small-boned Chinese way. The only change I noticed in him since our last meeting was a gold tooth cap, but I didn't offer congratulations.

"Outside your beat, aren't you?" I suggested.

"A little. I hope you didn't move to Kuala Lumpur to get away from me?"

"No. The thing I like about this town is roads going in every direction. There's always one that will have escaped a police block. You get a cooped-up feeling on an island."

He laughed.

"I've a few questions about a crashed plane, Mr. Harris. The Gemas police called me in on a little matter and I was rather led to the plane, you understand?"

"No, I don't."

"Well, the dead men were found in the Gemas road, actually. Three of them. Stolen jeep. No identification on the deceased of any description. We haven't found out who they were at all. The only thing we did find was that they had been seen in a rubber estate near the Bahau airstrip where you had that unfortunate pile-up. By an observant Tamil. You follow?"

"Certainly not."

"Dear me," said Kang gently. "Well, actually, what I want to know is why you were going toward Gemas at speed in your Mercedes shortly after the air crash?"

"Was I?"

"According to a bus driver. He's a Communist and thinks a Mercedes is antisocial."

Just the old Harris luck.

"He took the number. Smart of him, considering the speed you were traveling at. Over a hundred, the bus driver estimated. Were you, by any chance, chasing the jeep?"

I know my Kang. He'll stretch out the law to its maximum on occasion, but he does like being in the picture. And when you try to keep him out it's only trouble in the end.

"Yes," I said.

"Why?"

"The characters in it shot our plane down."

"Ah," said the Inspector. "So you took the law into your own hands again?"

"The law wasn't exactly available in those minutes. I don't have a telephone in my car. Maybe I should get one put in."

"You gave chase. What happened?"

"We caught them."

"And then?"

"Then they left the road and crashed. They were all dead so we came back to Kuala Lumpur. And I didn't report it. It was foolish of me, but I didn't think it would do any good. I wanted not to be disturbed just then."

"Because you had the Resident of Bintan staying with you?"

[42]

"Yes."

"And you think this was an attempt to assassinate him?"

"I'm not sure."

"Nor am I, where you're involved. Mr. Harris, I think I should tell you that we found a bullet imbedded in the chassis of the jeep. From a Webley. Do you have a Webley that I could hand over to our ballistics expert?"

"Let me think," I said.

"By all means. Take your time."

He smiled. This was real trouble. I could only gamble now. The little incident of the plane had seemed so far in the past I'd almost put it out of mind, as something over. But of course the local police wouldn't ask for help from Singapore until every avenue of their incompetence had been explored, and that deliberately.

"No Webley," I said.

"In that case the jeep must have been in other battles. I can't of course, see you closing with unarmed men and shooting them off the road. But it is curious that you should have had both the windscreen and the rear window of your Mercedes replaced recently."

"Who says that?"

"Oh, not your garage. They have been very loyal. But a garage has to get replacements from somewhere. In this case the Mercedes depot is in Singapore. They supplied the articles in question by direct sale to an unidentified purchaser. An unusual arrangement. And I had a look at your car this morning. Considerate of you to have parked it just outside. They've done a very good job at your garage, but it's been done recently. Somehow, to me, a smashed rear window suggests a gun fight, perhaps a running gun fight. High drama on the public highway, in fact."

I looked at Kang and then said:

"You win."

He nodded.

"I thought I would."

"Are you charging me?"

"I don't have a court case yet, Mr. Harris. The prosecutor these days is very stuffy. And you have the money for an unscrupulous lawyer. You would get off."

"So I would. That's a relief. What more do you want to know that I'd say in court had been got out of me by police brutality?"

"Did you identify any of these men?"

"No. I didn't even see them until they were dead. The one in the back kept taking pot shots at us. Very nasty it was, too. I've got their guns up at my house. You can have them and I'll put in a plea of self-defense. Czech rifles. One with a fancy telescopic sight that cost a lot of money."

"So you did shoot the jeep off the road?"

"Not exactly. It was a by-product of the battle."

"You were driving so I take it that the actual shooting was done by your very able assistant?"

"Under my orders. I'm the boss. The criminal responsibility is mine."

"So it is, Mr. Harris, so it is. Well, perhaps we can regard all this as part of the little wars which are going on around us all the time. Only remember this, in our present circumstances in this country, the police are not neutrals in the little wars. Our interests are not entirely focused on Tong feuds. You should recognize your allies and use them."

"I suppose I should. I've got used to looking after myself."

Kang had stood, but he stared down at me.

"Yourself, Mr. Harris? In this case? I wonder. We get wind of rumors sometimes. We had police at the airport to cover the arrival of a British Resident. We didn't want him to die on Malaysian soil."

I got up, too.

"Kang, what do you mean by that?"

"Just a rumor. With no facts to go on, and therefore I can say no more."

He went out. When I was sure Kang was clear of the outer office I summoned Ohashi on the intercom.

"Did you put that Webley back in the compartment of the Mercedes?"

The boy said:

"No, Mr. Harris. A Colt this time."

The Dog is a nice club. I don't know where it got that name, back in the dim ages of pre-two-world-wars perhaps. Officially it is the Selangor Club, and it sits on its own Padang where overheated idiots still sometimes play football, a hangover from more gracious times and the long short stories of Somerset Maugham. The Japanese made a small hole in the roof with a tiny experimental bomb, then patched this over and used the place as a whorehouse for officers only. After their departure it returned to a more innocent function as a boozer with Saturday night dances and a very mixed membership. There is once again a bar ladies are not allowed into, though they are fighting this.

I eat there about two nights a week, for the delicate Oriental insult keeps my cook up to scratch. It also gives me the illusion of having a social life, something I've not been too strong on in recent years. Every now and then on these evenings I find myself in the company of someone I wouldn't tolerate for five minutes in Singapore, an old hand who burbles in his cups about yesterdays, but up here I listen with a surprising blandness, the new man feeling his way in. Mostly though there is little nostalgia for lost power, just cheerful fellows out on salaried appointments with their wives who have begun to live for the first time and are haunted by the sheer horror of an eventual return to Golders Green. The girls tend to play just a little at the old game of memsahib but nobody minds too much. Since one of my nights is Saturday

I even dance on occasion, the program here offering us the waltz, foxtrot, tango, and about every six numbers one of the new things for the lads and lassies straight out from home called "The Potato" or "The Streetwalker." During these, about six couples, sweating, move out on a large floor and more or less stand there making faintly obscene gestures with knees and elbows which embarrass them, egged on by a Chinese five-piece band that would rather be somewhere else. By eleven the men-only bar is packed with chaps who have deserted their women.

I didn't hear myself paged for a long time in the din. Then it came quite clearly.

"Mr. Hallis? Mr. Hallis on telefoam, please."

The decor is newish, which means that we've got pink mirrors and form-fitting seats, too. The phones aren't in boxes any more, but in a hooded row and you stand as at a snack counter, not able to hear much that is being said on your line. It was a bad line, too.

"I can't get your name," I shouted. "Who's calling?"

An insect voice scraped away, faded and then suddenly chirped in my ear, very loud.

"Gissing here! Charles Gissing!"

"Yes, I've got that. Harris speaking."

"I've been trying to get you all day!"

"Sorry, I was up in Bentong. Didn't look in at my office and I haven't been home yet."

"I'm afraid I've got very bad news. I'm . . ."

"Can you speak up?"

He tried to, but a couple of women came by the potted palms and one of them was almost shouting.

"No, Madge, I simply won't be party to this. And I'm really surprised you asked me. He's old enough to be your father. And what about your husband?"

"Well, what about him?" Madge shouted back.

[46]

"Is that you, Gissing?"

"Yes. Did you hear me?"

"No. What the hell is all this?"

"John. He's dead."

The band started one of the new numbers. For just a minute I leaned on the counter.

"How?"

"Shot himself. Last night."

"What . . . ?"

"His Pathan servant found him. Do you remember the Pathan?"

"Yes. Charles, you know damn well John didn't shoot himself!"

"I can understand your feeling. It was mine, too. But it was at his desk. His own gun, everything. The police say . . ."

"I don't give a damn what the police say."

"Harris, there was cause, I can tell you."

"I know that! It doesn't alter the fact that John didn't kill himself."

"This is a terrible line. I can't go into things. But the point is that under the circumstances we opened John's will. Do you understand?"

"Yes."

"We were looking for any kind of instructions. You see, there was no note."

"I'm not surprised!"

"What? It was Lil we were thinking of. And that's in the will. I mean, what he wanted done. You're her guardian and trustee until she is twenty-one."

I stared at the polished formica backing in front of me.

"Did you get that, Harris?"

"I got it."

"It appears to be a new will, just drawn up. Did he speak to you about this?"

"No."

"Maybe he was going to write."

"Maybe."

"The thing is . . . Ursula and I are at our wit's end. Lil's with us, of course. We brought her over at once."

"How is she?"

"That's just it. She doesn't show anything. Of course it may be shock. But to have John's child showing nothing . . ."

"Child isn't the word I'd have used."

"No, maybe not. The thing is we're not . . . really in a position . . ."

"You want me to come over and assume my responsibilities?"

"Yes. Could you?"

"Right away. On the first plane I can get. I think that's tomorrow. I'm not sure."

"I'll send a government launch over to Latuan."

"Do that."

"I say, Harris, we're most grateful. I mean, Ursula will be, too. You'll stay with us, of course?"

"Thanks. But no, the rest house."

"Are you sure?"

"That would be best."

"Well, it's for you to say. The funeral's tomorrow. I'm afraid there is no question of waiting until you arrive."

There isn't, in the tropics.

"Gissing, who is your chief of police, again?"

"Manson. I'm sure you met him when you were over."

"Probably. Hasn't he been a bit hasty in deciding it was suicide? I'd say murder. I'd suggest you tell Manson to look again."

I turned away from the booth to bump into the florid-faced local manager of French-owned oil-palm estates.

"Oh, there you are, Harris. Bertie wants us all to go on to his place for a noggin. Coming?"

"No. Not tonight."

I had taken the Ford to Bentong. A Mercedes is something you want to savor by avoiding continual use, that way you keep the joy. But I wasn't going to feel the joy in my drive tonight. I did the change-over at the garage, brought out the big car, took it around to the house steps, and then went in to pack. Chow appeared in the bedroom door. He has a kind of instinct which tells him when another sudden departure is about to happen.

"Many clothes?" Chow wanted to know.

"I'll take a couple of cases."

"Where you go?"

He always asks and sometimes gets an answer.

"Bintan."

"No good, Bintan."

I didn't probe the reasons for this judgment. Chow's experience is limited and that walled about by solid prejudice against the unknown. He was born in Ipoh and once went to Singapore, where he had his wallet pinched. Anything across water is highly suspect and my trafficking on the high seas a kind of lunacy. He is one of the few Chinese I've ever met who appears never to give the old motherland a single thought and I like this in my house.

He took over the packing. When I opened my suitcases nothing would be missing. I put washing things into a waterproof bag, suddenly knowing how much I didn't want to go to Bintan where John was dead and Lil was waiting. I didn't want to think, either, of new responsibility toward the girl, though somewhere at the edge of consciousness was a kind of prevision of what the long flight to England was going to be like, Lil and me side by side on a plane that came down at

Bangkok, Calcutta, Cairo, Rome, with the airport rituals at each stop and no talk all the way, no talk at all, Lil rigid within herself, immune to my generation, sealed in her own. Why had John put down my name? I knew, though I wasn't going to look at it.

Chow carried the bags out to the car while I had just one small whisky for the road, needing that slight artificial warmth in my stomach. Then I went down the steps to find Ohashi sitting in the front passenger seat of the Mercedes.

"There are times when you're too psychic," I said. "How the hell did you know I was going off?"

"I am in office when phone comes from Bintan."

"What were you doing in the office on Saturday?"

"Work."

"Why the overtime? You're not a director yet."

Ohashi smiled.

"But I await privileged day."

I got in behind the wheel.

"Sure of yourself. I'm not taking you to Singapore. I'll run you home."

"I wish to come to Bintan."

"Wish again. This is a personal visit, not business."

"Mr. Harris, not good for you to go alone."

We slid down the hill.

"Is it my physical or spiritual good you're thinking of?"

"Physical, perhaps."

"Don't tell me you've been hearing things about Bintan, too?"

"Yes."

"From whom?"

"Captain of your junk. Kim Sung."

"He's an old rumor-monger. Time we retired him."

"I do not think so."

"Kim Sung is one of the reasons why I moved up here. Singapore was too handy for him. He was always popping into

[50]

the office. And it doesn't help brass-plate respectability to have a pirate visiting you regularly."

"Pirate so useful man in troubled days," Ohashi said.

I braked in front of the wobbly-looking four-story Chinese hotel in which Ohashi had a two-room nest.

"Here you are," I said.

"There is no need to go in. My bag packed and in boot with yours."

He looked glued into that seat beside me. I told him he could bring the car back from Singapore and drove on into the night, soon with headlights tunneling through dark arcs of trees which pressed close to the road. I was glad to have the boy along. It kept me from talking to myself out loud. I do sometimes, driving a car fast, having long conversations with my taciturn Ka. Psychiatrists wouldn't think it a good sign at all. On occasion I sing like a maniac, Chinese tunes of my own invention. I got my ear in for them as a boy in Shanghai.

"Where do you stay in Bintan, Mr. Harris?"

"The rest house. Why?"

"So. I phone you every day. For business matter."

"Just do what you think best and don't bother."

"I still phone."

It turned out that I had twenty-four hours to wait in Singapore before I could get a Malayair Viscount night flight to Latuan. There wasn't a private plane available which would undertake the nine hundred miles over water. I set the Mercedes with its nose pointing back to Kuala Lumpur, got Ohashi in behind the wheel and practically shoved him off. Then I went to a hotel and from it to see Russell Menzies.

Russell's offices are just off Raffles Square and he is almost always in them because he has no home life. These are by no means the usual legal chambers: they have japaned-black deed boxes, their place on one wall taken up by an enormous beer cooler which he bought secondhand from a supermarket. He

[51]

keeps this well-stocked. He lives on rivers of ice-cold Tiger beer and ham sandwiches and was having breakfast when I arrived.

When he saw me he lifted his feet off the top of his desk, groaning from the effort. He was, if anything, fatter. If ever a man's way of life invited a coronary Russell's did. The place was thick with cigar smoke which hadn't been sucked out by an extractor fan he was too lazy to switch on. Air conditioning he scorned as the road to pneumonia in the tropics.

"Hello, Paul. Been expecting you. Beer?"

"So you heard about John?"

"On the morning news. That's a bit of a hoo-ha blowing up, isn't it?"

"I'm not concerned with that side."

"Aren't you? Sit down, man. I hate to see anyone inviting fallen arches."

I sat down.

"Shot himself, did he?" Russell said.

"No."

"Now, now, calm down. I thought you'd be striking an attitude. Good old John. Wouldn't do a thing like that. Why not, eh? Every reason, from what I hear."

"Except one. John never ran away from anything."

"We all get tired."

"Not that tired."

"You knew him, I didn't. But speaking as a legal type I'd say we had all the ingredients of suicide. Career at an end."

"Russell, let's get personal. Supposing you were disbarred here in Singapore. And all that money you've salted away for a Scottish retirement you'll never risk melted overnight in some phony tin deal. Would you walk out? You'd be so damn mad at life you'd go on fighting it."

"At my age?"

"Yes."

"Well, I believe you love me. It's made my day. I said have a beer."

He lumbered over to the box, lifting the lid, peering down.

"Carlsberg, McEwans, Fowler's Wee Heavy, Budweiser or the local pale yellow you-know-what?"

"Pale yellow."

"It's an odd taste, isn't it? Becomes an addiction."

We drank out of the bottles. Russell kept breaking his tumblers. He sat down again. He was going to need a wider chair soon.

"So it's private investigator Harris who is going off on this trip? I take it you are going off?"

"Yes."

"What's Bintan like as a place to die in?"

"I've told you, I'm not getting mixed up in any political situation."

"So Harris turns over a new leaf? I thought you'd begin to rot up in K.L. They tell me you're giving cute little dinner parties by candlelight, too. Malaysia's own political host. Everything manipulated over the right kind of wine."

"It's too early in the morning for this," I said.

"Maybe it's too early in the morning to know that Boots Kinsley got back from his Japanese engagements last night? Arrived off the plane breathing through his nose to find his victim dead. I wonder what he'll do now? Go after the girl probably."

I was on my feet.

"Like hell he will! What hotel?"

"The tourist trap."

He shouted at me when I was at the door:

"You should learn to finish your beer, you idiot!"

The place I reached by taxi has had three face lifts in recent years and still looks like yesterday. The palms out in front make a noise as if they had asthma. The reception clerk was harassed over a cruise ship at anchor out in the roads and had to look up the suite number. He was young, but perhaps had an Oriental dislike of the guitar. I went up in the lift and along a passage reminiscent of faithless wives up to no good on an escape from a rubber estate. There were even shoes and high heels sitting side by side outside doors in the good old British tradition. I knocked on one of the doors and was told to come in.

I don't know what I'd been expecting, possibly a sitting room completely staffed with secretaries, impresarios, and teen-agers in negligees. All I got was Boots Kinsley on a sofa eating his breakfast.

I'd had enough photos shoved at me in the papers for instant recognition. He had long thin legs encased in some kind of tropic-weight shine and a bare chest without a hair on it. All the hair was up top in that pageboy-with-garden-shears cut. He had black eyebrows and smallish black eyes under them. The rest of his face looked like a face, not totally unpleasing, which surprised me. He had stopped chewing to say through toast:

"No autographs for the over-thirties. Buzz."

I shut the door. The chewing started up again while he looked around him, perhaps for a telephone. It wasn't handy.

"I buy my protection by the thousand quid's worth," Boots said. "I just traveled a little ahead of it this time. But I can still call in the local cops. Exit. I'm masticating."

Boots had won over the intelligentsia by his wit, but he wasn't wasting any of it when his press agent wasn't around. I was beginning to get more of his attention.

"Am I supposed to know you?"

"No."

"Good. I don't want to. And I don't like being stared at free. Something on your mind?"

"Yes. What it costs to sock you on the jaw. About twenty thousand pounds."

"Cheap at the price."

"I'm a fairly rich man. And there are no witnesses this time."

I moved. Boots gave up his breakfast and put the sofa between us. His eyes flicked about the room. There was no paid assistance available. Then the French windows opening onto a balcony gave him an idea.

"Don't try to make it," I said. "You wouldn't get there."

"Are you some kind of nut?"

"I'm a friend of Sir John Harpen."

That made him unhappy.

"You get out! Go on! I can make a noise, can't I?"

"The world hears you doing it."

"The Harpen thing's off, see?"

"Because he's dead?"

"I came down here to say it was off. Before I knew."

"I'm supposed to believe that?"

"Believe it, or don't. I flew down to fix it."

He had thin arms pushed out against the back of the sofa. I wasn't going to hit this boy. I wasn't going to do anything to him.

"Patching up the Boots Kinsley image?" I suggested. "A bit late. You'll find you've quite a job on your hands. A lot of people are going to say we've seen a kind of murder by guitar player."

"Shut up!"

"Have you checked your record company shares recently? I'd say they're teetering for a fall. And if I had any I'd be onto my broker for a quick sale. Before the general panic starts. I don't think you're going to be able to patch up the image in time, Kinsley. Not by any withdrawal of an action against a dead man."

"I didn't know he was dead, I tell you!"

"All right, you didn't know. But it will still hit your bookings. And the minute the screaming stops you've had it.

There are plenty of others with your sound just waiting to take over."

He pushed his body in against the back of that sofa, watching me.

"Finish your breakfast," I said. "I'm going. There's just one thing you'd better understand. Don't try ever to get near Lil again. I'll travel fast to wherever you are if you do try it."

FOUR

I WENT through passport control into the waiting lounge which is a feature of all international airports, a kind of limbo between the solid world and being airborne, where you are already segregated and parceled for transit even though you still have to wait for six hours while they're tightening up that engine someone found was about to fall out of a wing. There were a lot of us waiting in the small hours of the morning beloved of air companies, flights scheduled for London, Tokyo, 'Frisco, Brisbane and the little island of Latuan. Every one of us in that huge place had been converted to air travel some time ago but most of us still hated it. People sat about with the terrible nonchalance of the possibly damned in a new type of air-conditioned purgatory, trying to pretend that they weren't thinking about a long record of their sins. The very young had the best act, perhaps from fewer sins, sprawled in suspended boredom. And the kids, of course, were innocent and peevish.

I walked up and down while I still could, pausing at a bookstall for a thriller which had nothing about airplanes in it, then moving on to the gay little room with big windows where only the bartender seemed completely carefree. I wasn't driving and a double whisky was all right.

The 'Frisco flight was called and I watched a full booking go off across tarmac, single file mostly, all with a certain urgency on them, as though the only thing to do is get into that tin cigar quickly without any staring at the outside. And they are damn small for what is expected of them. It would probably have been much better for the tensions of our age if it had been possible to speed up the zeppelin. To my mind there is a huge area of potential medical research as yet untouched in a consideration of air travel as one of the major contributory factors to the vast increase of coronary disease. A character like Russell, who has never been in an airplane and doesn't intend to be airborne at any time in his future, continues to live unscathed though subjected to almost all of the other new stresses and with a bloodstream in which globules of fat are practically squeezing out the blood corpuscles. He's the best ad for sea travel, total physical inertia, and unlimited quantities of beer as aids to longevity, that I've ever seen.

The 'Frisco plane took off with the usual unpleasantly sharp angle of jet ascent and I went out of the bar to be stopped just outside the door by the spectacle of the most beautiful woman in Borneo sitting on a settee facing me. I don't like these competitive titles for pulchritude much and after each Miss World has been crowned I see a better-looking specimen behind the counter at the local Woolworth's. But this girl had deserved the all-in Borneo title for much more than a decade.

I had met her once in Bintan. She was a Princess, if you use the term loosely, the divorced sister of Abdul el Badas, the Sultan. And looking at her now I could remember that first meeting, going into a palace reception with John and seeing the Sultan's sister with the kind of light about her that real beauty, aided by diamonds, seems to attract, almost an aura. She had then been wearing a gold-worked Bintan sarong and baju, the short-waisted blouse, with a single scarlet hibiscus (plucked from the garden hedge) over one ear which said her love life was all right, in the local language of flowers. She was now wearing a silver-worked Kelantan sarong and white baju, with jade in her ears and on her hands and no flower of any color. Her jet hair looked as though it had undergone the usual stinky coconut-oil treatment for high gloss though it was probably some exclusive Paris spray set. Her lips, on that faintly gold-dust skin, were an unfashionable deep peony red. She was smoking a cheroot.

We had been introduced in Bintan and talked for fifteen minutes. It was something I remembered but there didn't seem any reason why she should, though I hovered hopefully for a moment until I was looked at. Linau's eyes are Korean amber set above just slightly Mongolian cheekbones, cool eyes which assessed my age, physique, and other accessories and then returned to the glowing tip of rolled tobacco leaf. It was a look which had taken her around the world several times on her own with as much privacy as though accompanied by bodyguards and three private secretaries.

Her divorced state really wasn't surprising. Very few husbands could be expected to endure for long such a continuous reminder of man's unworthiness. It would be not unlike having the Mona Lisa over your living-room mantel, a source of fantastic pride, perhaps, but all those burglar alarms meant you would never have a moment's real peace. Also, and worn as a kind of extra ornament all the time, was the strong suggestion of a very sharp intelligence, often unbecoming in a woman, but not here. Linau's brothers might be pirates gone soft, but she was pure Dyak, with the blood of gay sea killers still active in her veins.

I knew that she had once painted in Paris—John had owned one of her pictures—bold, Gauginesque splashes of hard color, the paintings beginning to sell well to collectors when she stopped, apparently bored. She now lived mainly in Bintan but was almost as subject to sudden travel as I am and there was an unconfirmed rumor that she was the only woman ever to have risked the rock-death dive at Acapulco. She had also spent almost a year in Reykjavik, dark and disruptive among all those sun-starved blondes.

I got a surprise then. Linau stood. She wasn't more than five-feet-two, light-boned. She didn't smile.

"How are you, Mr. Harris?"

Royalty, of course, have trained memories for people. We went into the bar. She sat on a stool. The sarong crackled, stiff cloth, a thousand dollars' worth. Linau's voice might have got the way it was from a prolonged screaming into a wind, a broken contralto. Her accent was precise, neither English nor American, international in the real lingua franca.

"We must both be suffering from the same shock," she said.

"You heard here?"

"No, in Hong Kong. I decided to come home. John was a close friend of mine."

I hadn't known that. The amber eyes were watching me.

"Is that child a fool?" Linau asked.

"I wouldn't call her that."

"John talked of you. Has he left the girl in your care?"

The question surprised me.

"So it would seem."

"I don't envy you the role."

"It's going to take some getting used to."

She drank whisky. Everyone in the place was looking past me at Linau. I felt it slightly exhibitionist to travel in airplanes wearing a sarong. Had she arrived in Reykjavik decked out like this under sables?

"You've been abroad again?"

She shook her head.

"Only Hong Kong."

Just two bus rides to a local big town.

When it was time to go out to the plane I still noticed that it was a rather beat-up Viscount with a lot of chipped paint. We went in the front entrance and sat side by side. The seats were booked-up there and we weren't booked together, but Linau just looked at the stewardess without smiling and one or two other people without smiling and we were together. Very soon after takeoff more whisky arrived. If the Princess had ever been a devout Mohammedan she had long since given up all idea of making the holy pilgrimage.

There are some beautiful women no sensible man could ever see himself coming home to. The great courtesans of all ages must have had this quality, nothing mysterious, just a label saying they were no one's personal property. The insult to the male ego implicit in this is provocative, practically an affront to a masculine dominance of the world, a comment on it which doesn't change the basic situation, only inserts the sound of clear, cool laughter. There are, fortunately, very few Linaus and an increase of their incidence would be as lethal to a stable, settled living as the super bomb.

It was a moment for obituary talk, that deliberate dehumanizing of the deceased which can push our friends firmly out into the night which has claimed them. Linau didn't offer this. There was no tribute, gracious from a member of the reigning house, to John's services to Bintan. She might have been really thinking about him. She lit another cheroot, a rough smoke for that time in the morning.

"I met your brother in Singapore, Mr. Harris."

This was news which still didn't surprise me. My brother never used to discuss the women with whom he made contact.

"Twice," Linau added. "He was a hard man."

"I'd say tough."

"And you are not tough?"

"Not at all. I'm adapting myself to change out here like a chameleon."

"Your brother would not have done that?"

"I doubt it. He believed that the world belonged to the rough."

"You don't?"

"What I believe is changing. I'm backing Malaysia."

"So I heard," Linau said.

A stewardess came by our seats to ask if we were comfortable. Linau looked at the girl without saying anything and we were alone again. The cabin lights dimmed for those who wanted to use a portion of this dark in seat-cramped sleep. I found myself wondering about Linau's influence over her brother and his plans to keep oil company revenues flowing straight into the family pockets. He wouldn't be the first potentate out in these parts to dance to a sister's tune. This girl hopped about the world but she always kept coming home and it might be more than personal feelings which was bringing her home right now. John's death could precipitate a real crisis in Bintan, or it could be part of something already started. I tried out a small-caliber bomb.

"A plane John and I were in was shot down in Malaya."

Linau didn't move for a moment, then she turned in her seat, her whole body. The surprise seemed real.

"You know this for certain?"

I told her what happened. At the end she suggested, as John had, that I might be the target. I gave her the answer I had given him and it seemed an even better one now.

"You don't believe John killed himself, Mr. Harris?"

"I'm sure he didn't."

"How can you be so sure?"

"I suppose in the way we know our friends."

Linau was looking out of the window again.

"So much was happening to him."

"He would have wanted to go on facing things."

"You can't know! It's impossible."

Her hands were together, held tightly.

"Even the most fortunate . . ." she began.

"Yes?"

"I can be very tired, sometimes."

Just like old Russell in Singapore. I didn't know whether Linau had been aiming for the tragic note but she didn't make it. This girl came from a long line of characters whose idea of bliss was to die in bloody sea fighting before rheumatism set in. And none of them had tired easily. Her brother might be decadent but I didn't think she was, only an experimenter with decadence, who went her long journeys to do this and then came back again to the pirate base. There was no malaise of soul here, just a very fortunate extrovert who, when she wanted a man, put the right colored flower in her ear to say so. And in parts of the world where the flower signs wouldn't work there were other signal flags she could run up. She inhaled that cheroot smoke, too. I'd been watching her do it.

Linau ended talk by putting her head back against the seat and closing her eyes. After a little it looked like sleep. She also looked very beautiful. It would be impossible ever to love this woman. She had no mirror to hold up for the reflection love demands, but you could certainly want her.

Our only landfall was the point of Borneo just above Sambas and we reached it in moonlight, a shadow line marking a frame edge to glitter sea. There was no real suggestion of the vast island which lay behind, bigger than Spain, almost a continent, its central portions still unexplored, its fringes marked by little patches of exotic history. Just to the north of our position white rajas had ruled for a hundred years, their feudal pomp recognized by Queen Victoria who granted a tough British adventurer the title of Highness. Farther north still, the British North Borneo Company had hung on as commercial and civil administrators of a vast territory long after such anachronisms had disappeared everywhere else in the world. And while all this was going on the tribes up in the interior ate their enemies and still did in some places. For extroversion the place was a psychiatrist's nightmare.

I got out of my seat and went back to be nice to that poor little stewardess.

Yesterday's British Empire seems to have stuck to a pattern, perhaps worked out in Whitehall, when building capitals of small colonial states. And not only in the tropic Far East, either. I can remember my surprise coming into Sierra Leone to see once again the same town, bazaar quarter, zinc-roofed bungalows, the slightly pompous administrative buildings and a spired Anglican cathedral.

Bintan is prettier than average. It sits on a curved bay which is also the mouth of the river, a small bund of colonnaded buildings which look bright from a distance but turn out to be the usual peeling plaster. On rising ground bungalows stick out timber elbows into hard light, their main bulk hidden in green jungle which rolls back from the houses and climbs to a bread-knife edge sawing away at a hazed blue sky. Near the shore, but only there, are some palms and casuarinas. The Anglicans didn't manage a spire in this town, the Muslims got in first with a minareted mosque which has an electric-blue dome. The Sultan's palace, like a rococo Blenheim, sends out huge, pompous ocher-washed wings, and is set apart in an area stripped of shade trees, glaring and aggressive.

I sat forward of an awning feeling the bounce of the launch on a crisp, only lightly whipped morning sea, watching the town come at us. For me all these places offer an appealing suggestion of a tidy pattern which can be known in its entirety. And this is the real opposite of urban living, a capital which is still a village, where a launch coming is a minor event and a steamer practically fiesta. Such a place contains you, of course, but it is also an insurance against the terror I sometimes feel when walking alone at the bottom of glass canyons. Any man settling for a Bintan is certain soon to feel lost away from it, thrust out into a vast indifference where the best you can hope for is a certain uneasy familiarity with a few small cells in a monstrously humming hive. I know I couldn't really live in a place like Bintan but the idea of doing so remains as a recurrent temptation, an alternative to my patterns which would be enormously cosy for the ego, if very bad for initiative.

Linau, no sun worshipper, was back under the awning. We hadn't breakfasted together at Latuan. I think she was having a bath while I ate bacon and eggs. The government launch Gissing had sent didn't turn out to be specially favored treatment either, for word got around and at least thirty travelers for Bintan decided not to wait for the daily steamer service and piled in with us, unabashed by royal company. There was cargo, too, and a few feet away from me a large crate of hens who hated travel, scraggy specimens who stuck their heads through holes in rattan for a two-and-a-half-hour protest demonstration.

From the water Bintan didn't suggest a busy capital, the harbor nearly empty, only three or four anchored junks with no life stirring on them at all, as though they were mothballed. The town had four streets running inland and rising slightly toward the hills. None of these were troubled by any acute traffic problem and the people in them weren't hurrying to anything. Quite a crowd had gathered to watch us come in, middle-of-the-day betel chewers, and as the launch engines cut out I heard a rattletrap bus backfire a protest into windless heat and a dog barking.

I saw Charlie Gissing climbing out of a car which had just come to a stop up on the Bund. He was one of those characters you don't forget mainly because they are so unmemorable, rather short, overweight, his face pudgy and pink under blond hair which hasn't stood up well to wear and tear. He had a canine desire to be loved which sat unhappily on top of snatched-at bids for official dignity and it was easy to see how he had got lost in Bintan.

His superiors would want it. When promotion was on the agenda at the conference table, and Charlie's name came into it, one of the gray men would issue a rationed smile and that would be that. Charlie really belonged to the topee era, but born too late for it, when the nonentity could top himself off with that huge exclusive status symbol and under it contrive to face his world. In our time of bare heads in the tropics he was lost and knew it.

I watched him come down the jetty. Shorts and bush shirt, put on crackling with starch only a few hours earlier, already had a slept-in look. He carried a walking stick and prodded with it the cracks between stones. He peered down most of the time, as though the thought that he was now Acting Resident of Bintan wouldn't let him straighten his neck. He was also probably feeling real grief for John.

In reply to my hand signal I got an inefficiently executed empire builder's wave of the ash stick and Charlie kept his head up to glance along the launch at the other occupants. We were near enough for me to see his face and on it came a look of sheer panic. He was staring at Linau.

After what seemed a long time his hand came up in a cap-less salute and then stayed hovering about his forehead while the wind lifted thin strands of hair. It was, of course, possible that Linau's homecomings rated a seven-gun tribute which it was the Resident's duty to lay on, but I didn't think that was the trouble. He was just horrified to see Bintan's most cele-brated woman about to step once again on her native soil.

Linau did that very gracefully, accepting a natural preced-ence over her brother's impatient subjects, then waiting for her luggage to be handed up. If she said anything to Charlie I didn't hear it, but she turned back to me, with a suggestion of that unsmiling stare so lethal to stewardesses and others.

"You must come to dinner, Mr. Harris. I'll give you a ring at the rest house."

Then she went up the jetty. I got ashore before the chickens but after the rest of the passenger list and by then Charlie had crept back into some kind of composure.

"Awfully good to see you," he said, as though he meant it.

"Sorry the launch was so crowded. It always happens. All the Bintanese over at the Latuan markets regard any boat from here as their own. The steamer ferry people get very cross about it. I hope you weren't uncomfortable?"

"Not at all. How are you, Charles?"

"Oh, all right, I suppose. Though things are in a dreadful state, as you can imagine. Dreadful. Is that all your luggage?"

I had to carry my cases to the waiting car. Charlie had a driver but his authority over the man seemed a bit uncertain and though the Malay behind the wheel turned his head to look at me he didn't get out to do anything about the bags.

"Ursula has coffee waiting," Charlie said. "We'll just go straight to the Residency."

"You're there now?"

He looked slightly guilty.

"Well, yes, I thought we'd better. The offices are there. And Lil wanted to get back. She couldn't be allowed to go alone, so Ursula and I packed a few things and came with her."

Ursula was having her time, however brief, as lady of the manor. She filled the role with the kind of dignity which waits for guests in a drawing room. Charlie and I got out under the pillared portico and went into a hall designed for coolness, plenty of space and plants in pots of the kind that can live permanently in shade, if under protest. Ursula was in one of those salons that appear hopeless for privacy, with doors and long windows everywhere and all of them open, but if you sit right in the middle you're so far from everything that there's a good chance your voice won't travel to listening ears.

She was right in the middle, under a ceiling fan. Air conditioning hasn't reached Bintan except at the oil company's domain. Her chair was one of a high-backed set that could have been a Colonial Office issue in 1890 and by some dubious miracle not yet eaten away by white ants. I had never known John to use this room which would have made the perfect setting for the kind of reception, with music behind palms, that I never attend. In front of my hostess was a coffee tray.

She rose, a tall woman, a head and a half above Charlie, suggesting at once an overlooked candidate for a British life peerage who is extremely cross she hasn't made it. Her too-long pongee silk dress was a comment on a life spent remote from any consciousness of contemporary Western fashions.

"Ah, Paul."

I hadn't, on previous visits, been elevated to close friendship with Ursula, but common grief is a great leveler and for the time being I was in the circle.

"We were so glad you could come at once. To help us with Lil."

That was my role defined.

"How is she?"

"In her room, poor child. She hardly leaves it. She has been rather strange about it all. Shock, I expect."

Ursula sank back into her throne from which she poured, gave me a cup, then asked: "Has Charles said anything?"

The Acting Resident rushed in to assure his wife that he had stuck by orders, which meant Ursula could begin at the beginning, which she did.

"Poor, poor John."

Three quarters of an hour later I was right in Ursula's picture which I took it was Charlie's, too, for all he did was make little noises of assent.

John had been found in the morning shot in his study, sitting at his desk, slumped against it. The gun had been his Colt automatic and the bullet had been discharged from close to his right temple, making a nasty entrance wound but no exit, the autopsy finding it lodged in a piece of skull. I gathered that things hadn't been neat at all. Ursula covered these details with a detached calm that would have been a credit to a police sergeant. For a little I thought I was in for one of those locked-room mysteries, for a key had been turned, but it was later found that the French windows only had slatted shutters pulled to and John's personal servant, the Pathan acquired in India, had got in that way to find him.

There had been no note and nothing about the desk or in it suggesting a man planning to step out of life and wanting to leave things tidy behind him. The recent will showed a personal estate of some seventeen thousand pounds which was larger than I had expected it to be, though certainly not enough to meet costs in a big libel action. He had died a man facing a sharp end to his life work, alienated from his daughter and about to be stripped of his cash reserves, though it still wasn't a combination of circumstances which suggested suicide to me. I didn't say this to Ursula; she wouldn't have liked her summing-up challenged.

We were interrupted by a servant in the way you are in palaces and residences, no shut door any security against them. This man was rather portly for a Chinese and I didn't remember him. His voice was thin and high, reducing dignity.

The Acting Resident had been summoned to the palace and the Sultan's Rolls was at the door to take him there. It was clearly a royal order. From the look which came on Charlie's face right then this was the first he had received since taking over new authority. Ursula's calm remained but under it was the sudden panic of a wife who is uneasy about a husband subjected to a vital test without warning.

"Oh, how tiresome for you, Charles. I wonder if this means lunch at the palace?"

He shook his head at once, as though the Sultan had an established reputation for being mean about free meals.

"Are you going to change, dear?"

"No."

Charlie should have accepted her suggestion here, instead of just looking surly.

"See you later, Harris."

That was almost gruff, the man of action off on another

round of duty, a reasonable exit rather spoiled by the look his wife sent after him. She would have organized the moment differently if I hadn't been on hand as a witness. We heard, distantly, a car door shutting and then a crunch of gravel. With an effort Ursula brought her attention back to me.

"Poor Charles," she said. "Everything is such a strain for him just now. He was so devoted to John."

"Yes."

"I'll take you to Lil."

We walked out into the hall and up a staircase which just missed being splendid. The curious feeling of dereliction persisted for me, as though the building had come to the end of its use and was aware of this before the occupants. Upstairs a vast long corridor bisected the house, lit by side passages like vents leading down to verandas. Everywhere were closed doors and most of the rooms beyond them would stay shuttered day and night. There were gilt mirrors filmed by blue damp at intervals on the walls, each with an attendant marble-topped whatnot on which sat Chinese vases no longer holding flowers. Ursula hesitated, as though she had to think to get the right door, then knocked.

The door was solid teak, massive, without ventilation slats. Ursula knocked again and turned a handle.

"Lil, dear? It's Mr. Harris to see you."

Her voice had assumed the rather grim sweetness of those who have never had much to do with the young and don't want to.

"Lil, you've locked this door!"

I wasn't as surprised as my hostess seemed.

"I can't understand it," she said. "I hope the child's all right? Lil!"

The answer from within must have been shouted; it was clear.

"Go away. I'm not seeing anyone."

"But Lil, Mr. Harris has come from Malaya . . ."

I asked to be allowed to handle things.

"You want me to go away, Paul?"

"Lil might like to see me alone."

"Oh. Very well. But she's never locked the door before. It's so odd. I'll meet you downstairs."

Ursula's retreat took time, almost a progress, the walk away of a tall, just slightly wobbly woman who has never in her life had to hurry any place and wouldn't like to have to do so. Watching her I wondered how she tolerated leaves home in England, for she was no fool and in the old country these days it must be borne in on her very forcibly indeed that she belonged in an era which had vanished. The main tenet of her creed, that it is the duty and privilege of an aristocratic minority to run Britain and half the world as well was not only discredited but had died and been buried, and without much pomp either. Ursula had been left in this relic of yesterday and moved through it like a chronic mourner for deceased authority. It was a Victorian mourning, too, prolonged and stylized and carrying an undertone of hypocrisy.

I didn't knock on the door.

"Lil, let me in."

"Why should I?" She shouted that. "I know what you'll say. I don't want to hear it! I know what you're thinking, too."

"I'm not thinking anything. I came here to help you."

"I don't need your help."

"Your father thought you did."

"My father . . ."

The silence went on for quite a long time.

"Lil, if you'll open the door I'll go away the moment you tell me to."

"Go away now!"

In me she expected to face an accuser. I couldn't shout

through wood that I was certain her father hadn't killed himself. It might have got that door open, but it could also have been overheard.

"Will you please leave me alone?"

Her voice was suddenly muffled.

"All right. I'll come back when you want me. I'm staying at the rest house. You can ring me there."

"I won't."

A moment later, as though to underline this, came noise from a portable, Boots calling the world on a record, telling Lil and others he had what she needed.

I went down one of the side aisles to a veranda. From out there I could have got to Lil by climbing over a couple of screen partitions, but decided not to. In the lower hall Ursula seemed to emerge from a nest of columns, and with just a faint air of triumph.

"She wouldn't let you in?"

"No. I'll try later."

We went into a small private sitting room which had once been Lil's mother's, where long ago there had been a despairing bid for a note of femininity, soon abandoned in an apartment with all the charm of a left-luggage repository. Ursula had inserted canna lilies, two pots of them, like tributes at a forgotten altar.

"What are you going to do now?"

"I'm not sure."

"Were you planning to take Lil on the afternoon boat for Latuan?"

"Not really. She won't be ready today. Tomorrow perhaps."

"I see. You'll stay for lunch, of course? I assumed you would and sent your bags to the rest house."

It was kind of her, but I declined a meal at the Residency. It had always been like eating in a museum, a vast dining room in Colonial Service apple green which seemed to put the emphasis on man's mortality in those moments when you were trying to build up your resistance against the inevitable. John, also, had never shown much instinct for choosing a cook, which is a matter of major importance in parts of the world where cooks are still the custom. As I remembered them meals in this house invariably suggested canteen issue made just slightly classy with parsley garnish. And the Chinese who ran the rest house had a flair for quite remarkable near-gastronomic effects with a chicken that had died naturally of malnutrition.

I asked to have a look at John's study and was told that Manson, the policeman, had locked the place up and wasn't letting anyone in.

"In that case I'll get on to the rest house."

"The car's not back yet, Paul."

"I'll walk."

"In the heat?"

But I wasn't really pressed to stay. Lunch alone with her husband would be much more interesting. Ursula didn't come with me beyond the door to her retiring room and I had a long solitary progress down to the portico. Out there, as though waiting to see me, was John's Indian bearer. I got a much deeper bow than I deserve.

The only languages I've learned are the ones I was more or less born to and Urdu isn't one of them. I remembered that this Pathan had acquired no Malay at all, was quite stubborn about it, which meant that he had been almost totally isolated in John's household, able to speak to his employer but very few others. There were Indians in Bintan, but only Tamils and because of this they were damn near untouchables. The Pathan had acquired a little English which he squeezed out painfully when it was absolutely essential.

"Sahib."

The old word, not often heard now.

"Shah Valli. Nice to see you."

"Yes, good so. Yes, Sahib."

The turban bent again and came up. His chiseled face had little loose appendages of fat about the jowls, but his eyes could still hold the terrible light of the warrior, and it was his eyes that were strange.

I blundered out a few words for the man's pain, which I knew was real, and those eyes changed. His mouth moved but he didn't produce speech. I was conscious of his plight, a retainer left alone with his world ended. There might be something I could do about that, to help him toward a new one, perhaps take him when I left with Lil. In Singapore there were many of his race, but he was old; you could see that under the erect dignity, that façade of control, perhaps too old for change.

"You go, Sahib?"

"Yes, to the rest house."

This seemed to trouble him, as though it threw some plan out of gear.

"I'll be back soon," I said.

And then Ursula's voice sounded down the hall.

"Shah Valli?"

Into the man's eyes came a look suddenly obliterating everything else. He hated to be summoned by a woman. But he went.

To walk at noon in the tropics is still the lunacy that Mr. Noel Coward once sang about, and in seconds I was sweating. The Residency grounds are large and took a long time to leave on foot, acres of those official gardens which have the look of a park where no one is allowed to picnic on the grass. The lawns appeared almost English until you were close enough to see a texture all wrong, a knitted pattern of bluish blades carefully watered and groomed into an imitation of the real thing. Along with the bougainvillaea and hibiscus were enormous round clumps of plumed pampas grass, someone's idea of horticultural dignity, and near the outer walls a magnificent fringe of monstrous jungle hardwoods which made a deep shade.

The road into town used this shade, and from it I could soon see the Sultan's palace, glaring at the sea. I walked past scattered bungalows, each with its patch of unkempt jungle for privacy, and on to a junction where the road into town is joined by another from the oilfields and the rest house. I turned into this, away from Bintan, a tunnel of airless shade I was glad to escape over the hump of a little hill.

The local apology for a hotel sits on its own isolated bay with a good beach behind it if you don't mind the sharks. It would make the perfect site for a tourist development which I hope never happens and isn't likely to, for the oil company has its own arrangements for visiting V.I.P.'s, a prefabricated building of extreme hideousness offering such un-Bintanese comforts as controlled air temperature at sixty-eight degrees which always gives me a cold in the head. In fact the oil company has everything for a life totally insulated against the local one, and they are busy now building their own jet strip.

The rest house looked like a planter's fifty-year-old idea of a setting for the gracious life, two stories, with verandas up and down and a number of newer attendant outbuildings in stucco for the staff. It had no welcome sign and no cars parked outside. I went up steps and across a wide porch into a moderately cool reception area which was vast and equipped with everything that was considered essential for the white man's comfort back in 1903. There were wicker chairs, copies of *Punch*, a few potted palms, a fan going but an air of great emptiness as though in waiting after curtain up for the first Tennessee Williams' character to come slouching in. There was a desk set in a recess and a rack for letters behind it, but the rack was empty and so was the cubicle. I rang a little punch bell.

On the third ring Lee Wat came through a door somewhere in a passage, an almost silent flopping toward me, but with his face illumined by a good host's joy at a new customer. He wore a white jacket and black pants, his head shaved and polished.

"Mr. Hallis? I no hear car coming?"

"I walked."

This startled him.

"So? Lunchings now?"

"Bath first."

"Sure, I fix. What you eat? Curry? Chicken? Cold ham? Salad? Clean salad, dip in purple water."

He meant I wouldn't get worms from his Chinese lettuce.

"Mr. Hallis, you Bintan before?"

The small town. They remembered you.

"Yes, I ate here when I could. I remember your cooking."

He grinned.

"You wanchee hot water?"

"Cold's fine. Where do I register?"

He got out the book. It was a big book which had been used a long time and was still only half full. I picked up a pen.

It was blown out of my hand. I was shoved up against the counter and held there by a sucking vacuum of blast, all in a silence. Seconds later sound came, the smack of it like a fist hitting my ears. The big frame building lifted, groaned and settled. Things fell off the walls. Lee Wat screamed.

There was other screaming, too, from the back quarters somewhere, women's voices. But the smell came from up above, first an acrid tang like firecrackers at a party, then something else, sweet and sickly.

The stair treads were covered with debris, the upper hall railing and banisters blown down all over them. I could hear a crackling of fire before I got up. Another long passage split the house, with teak doors on both sides of it. One of these had been blown off, the top mangled splinters, the timbers which had once held it blackened. The door lay half across the passage and I could see a shape on the floor in a bedroom.

The shape was surrounded by little smoldering fires, tiny flames, but was itself immune. Half a head was left, enough for me to know who it was. There was the turban, too, but not white any more.

Before I saw my bags intact on a stand near the veranda windows I knew that this was my room.

FIVE

"Go out and wait for me on the veranda," Manson said.

It was an order from the local police chief. I stepped over leaking hose pipes, glad to be getting clear of the racket inside the building. But even out in the open I kept on smelling burned flesh.

In about five minutes the policeman arrived with two glasses.

"You've had a bit of a shock, Harris. Here's your medicine."

It was brandy. He stood there staring down.

"Any idea why Shah Valli was trying to get into your room?"

"He wanted to see me."

"Why?"

"There was something on his mind. And we failed to communicate back at the Residency."

Manson sat. Wicker creaked. He had red cheeks, had red knees in shorts, and was overweight, with the look of a man who had once been much more so, an excess of skin for the flesh now beneath.

"Why try to see you in your room?"

"He could be sure of getting me alone. He saw me walk off to come here. He knew I'd want a bath as soon as I arrived. So I suppose he came on a bike a back way. Have you found a bike?"

"Yes."

"Then that's it and I'm a damn fool."

"In what way particularly?"

"Not catching on about that need to talk to me alone. I just played pukka sahib greeting faithful old native servant. And because of that he's dead."

"Pity," Manson said, with limited compassion. "He could, of course, have died because he was trying to contact you."

I looked out across the yard and toward the road with jungle trees beyond it. One of Lee Wat's undernourished hens had escaped confinement and was pecking for crumbs out in the dust. I asked Manson if he had any reason to suspect Shah Valli of knowing something about John's death.

"No, I didn't. I couldn't get a damn thing out of the man. He. was practically incoherent. I got an interpreter and that was worse. The old boy wasn't going to do any talking through him. Though I didn't think he had anything to tell us."

"I'm sure you were wrong."

"Nothing we can do about it now."

"Manson, do you believe that John was a suicide?"

He didn't look at me.

"Officially."

"What the hell do you mean by that?"

"What I say about something and what I think about it are quite often two different things these days. It all started when I began to realize I was being watched very carefully."

He still wouldn't look at me.

"Who by?"

"My own men. The only reason I can talk now is that you had the sense to choose a chair way down here and against a solid wall. Trained yourself to watch where you sit?"

"Yes. Do you know which men?"

"Two of what you might call my closest associates. But I've no proof, of course. And we have a smart little force. Fine discipline."

He laughed.

"When did all this start?"

"A year or two ago. Bintan suddenly stopped letting the world go by. You might even say we've got an emergent new nation in this little hole. All the result of oil. Before oil no one wanted to emerge at all. And the policeman's life was positively happy. Only the monthly kampong murder of an unfaithful wife and an occasional amuck. Comfortable routine. I can tell you I miss it. Now I look at my top sergeant and see someone quietly practicing for my job after the take-over of power."

"John never hinted that things were like this."

"It was his business not to. Didn't you notice that he hadn't had a leave for four years? Nor have I. No reliable British deputy any more. All the career boys decided to get off this sinking ship some time ago. Can't say I blame them. If I were younger I'd have done it, too. Ever hear of Bintan's freedom party?"

"I thought it was the local joke?"

"We laughed about it yesterday. Today I have to come well down a veranda out of earshot to talk to you. Also to tell you that if you're marked down for elimination in our happy little state there's only one thing I can really do. Give you good advice. Get to hell out on that afternoon boat with Lil. And start organizing your retiral now. I can keep you covered to the boat and onto it, but I can't give you more protection than that. None at all if you hang on in Bintan. The local chief of police now drinks brandy on duty."

He didn't look all that disintegrated to me.

"Why try to do me in?" I asked.

Manson turned and smiled. He had strong yellow teeth.

"Maybe because it's widely known that you're a nosy character. And just at the moment you're the kind of tourist to be discouraged. Or assassinated. Brought a gun with you?"

"No."

"Careless. I can't give you an issue, and you won't need it if you get on that boat."

"If I don't?"

"I'd say you'd need a gun. I can tell you where to get one on our local black market. A little Colt will cost you a thousand Malay dollars. We've got inflation in small arms, due to a troubled internal situation."

"You believe John was murdered," I said.

Manson made the wicker creak.

"Yes, I believe that. He was my good friend and I'm in charge of law and order here. Doesn't it make you sick? I'd clear out, Harris. This is no place for you to die in. You wouldn't even be defending your business interests. You can't help John."

"Are you just putting in time for your pension?" I asked.

He nodded.

"That's it. Though sometimes I wonder who the hell will pay it."

I watched him go down the veranda and near the main door to the lounge he was met by his top sergeant, apparently with a report. Manson listened, nodded and went down the steps, never looking in my direction. He gave a signal to the ambulance which moved off toward Bintan town. The sergeant bellowed for his boys and left, too, followed shortly by seven men of the volunteer fire brigade who rolled their hoses toward an empty truck and then climbed in. Very soon the rest house was left to a remarkable silence and in it I began to notice that I was hungry.

The kitchen in an establishment of this kind isn't one of the places the habitual eater out in the Far East goes into much, or for that matter in the West either. I saw the basin of permanganate my salad would have been dipped into, too dilute a solution to be more than a gesture, and I saw a lot else, all of it likely to turn a man into a home-lover prone to sudden sweeping surprise inspections of domestic culinary procedures. A good case could be made for an organized oriental attempt, via kitchens, to wipe out the last remnants of the white oppressor with food poisoning. Three women were in there, one of them weeping, and my appearance seemed to intensify general distress.

"A sandwich," I said.

This resulted in a second woman starting to cry. The spectacle of an unfeeling monster who could want to eat at a time like this was just too much for her. I could see her point, but my stomach has a tendency to recover from shock before the rest of me, so I found bread and cut it—after washing the knife—and located ham in the fridge. It was a club sandwich, three layers, and I took it back into the public parts of the building where there was a three-day-old copy of the *Straits Times* to wrap it in. There was also some beer in a case behind the reception desk and no sign of Lee Wat on guard. I helped myself to a couple of bottles, together with an opener, and headed for the beach where I could use the sea for my bath.

Like everyone else these days I've been conditioned into a drip-dry consciousness by the synthetic-fabrics business and though my houseboy at home takes this as a personal insult and won't allow it, the moment I start traveling I can't wash my body without washing as well everything that has been on it. So I did a little laundry down there at the burbling edge of tropic surf, bringing this back to smooth, hot rocks for a quick sun dry, and wearing only dark glasses for my meal.

Settled back against a heap of sand I was aware that what I was doing was probably foolhardy, that a man who has just missed being assassinated is well advised to keep on his trousers in case there is a follow-up attempt. But that beach had a swept empty innocence which was sedative in effect. Also, in my experience, planned murder which hasn't come off, or got the wrong victim, tends to result in a re-think of the general situation by the perpetrators, which allows for a little time out all round. At any rate I was taking it.

I stared at the South China Sea while almost white-heat evaporated salt damp from my skin. There was a comfortable little breeze which kept the air temperature down to a civilized eighty and a measure of composure began to seep back into me through pores.

There was plenty to think about and I tried to do it, marshaling facts like the "pro" detective in a whodunit, but I found my thoughts lurching away from what I expected of them toward a consideration of the human condition, starting with Manson's obvious terrible loneliness, and from there to John's, and moving on to Charlie's—for all he had Ursula—and ending up with my own. Nobody loved me in Bintan and not many outside the place. A realization of this has hit me hard in tightening circumstance before. I don't know whether it's a spur or not to see clearly, when you may depart this life at any moment, that this event would cause no real ripple anywhere.

John had been a better and much more useful man than I am and already he was as remote from continuing existence as the character whose public service has earned him yesterday's two-column obituary in the *Times* of London. I could make a duty visit to the place where they had buried a friend, but I didn't want to and knew I wouldn't. At the very back of my mind, in a far corner and covered by some pious sentiment, was the faintest feeling of resentment at the immunity of the dead, at their escape, leaving responsibility to the living. In this particular case Lil.

Lil was almost certainly lonely, too, without Boots, but she still had youth's wonderful confidence that the state is an unnatural one, a temporary product of circumstance from which you can escape into true love. You never escape into anything, though you have to be in your thirties before this becomes finally and totally apparent. It all boils down to the fact that if you haven't learned to live with yourself by halfway through life you haven't learned to live. It may be sad but it has to be faced.

As Manson said it would be pointless for me to die in Bintan, in which I had no stake, and only the interest of having the place, with its oil assets, added to the Federation of Malaysia. The obvious thing was to collect Lil, by force if necessary, and catch the afternoon boat, giving the police a ring to tell them of my plans and expecting the cover of their protection for a few hours. I had been promised this much. I ought to be sensible. But I never have been. A stubborn persistence in obvious folly is a kind of curse shared by nearly all Scotsmen who haven't elected to stay quietly at home.

I must have closed my eyes on this thought, a kind of amen, and when I opened them again I wasn't alone on that beach, Linau was about eight feet from me.

"What a sensible way to recover from an attempt to kill you, Mr. Harris."

I'm not a natural nudist and my efforts to get into a pair of underpants contained an element of panic. It was some time before I noticed her complete composure. The girl who went in for sarongs abroad chose brief shorts and a white open-necked shirt for casual wear at home, no ear flowers, no trimmings. Except for coloring she looked rather like one of those British railway station posters for the happy outdoor holiday life at Margate, the sexless beauty who only wants a game of handball on the sands with maybe some jolly dancing to follow. There was no sign of a cheroot.

"You took quite a bit of finding."

"Why the search?" I asked, half surly.

"It's my feeling you shouldn't linger in the area of the rest house. Are you catching the afternoon boat?"

"Everyone asks me that."

"And are you?"

"No."

"What's your reason for staying in Bintan?"

"Lil isn't ready to leave yet."

"That isn't a strong reason, Mr. Harris. What's the real one?"

[84]

"I haven't come on it yet."

"I see. If you must stay on, not here."

"Are you offering me a wing of the palace?"

"I wouldn't recommend that, either. But I have my own house here. You're welcome to share it."

I looked at her.

"Isn't there a public image of you that has to be maintained?"

"No. We're a relaxed community in some ways. Have you any cigarettes?"

I gave her one and we both sat down on the sand. She had a raffia handbag with a bulge in it that could be from one of Bintan's thousand-dollar Colts. I felt underdressed.

"You ought to go, of course. But if you must stay my house is the best place for you."

"Give me three reasons."

"It's guarded day and night. My cook is a Hailam, trained in curries. And I'm a charming hostess."

It sounded like the ideal permanency for the rough contemporary world, but I still wasn't greatly tempted.

"Thanks very much. I think I'll stay a free agent."

"Dangerous. You don't take advice, do you, Mr. Harris?"

"Only when I like it."

Linau had become just faintly angry. She had spent a good deal of her life terminating contacts, not trying to foster them, which made her almost clumsy now.

I got up and put on my trousers, then my shirt. I loaded my pockets.

"Where are you going?"

"To pay a business call on one of the leaders of your community. A Mr. Yin Tao."

She didn't like that at all, and there was no offer of a lift into town.

I got a hire car to come for me. The Chinese have acquired most of the trade in tropic Southeast Asia by ignoring the siesta hour and though Bintan looked sleepy enough I didn't expect that Mr. Yin would be resting. He conducted his affairs from the kind of headquarters which announce that the man who is really running things doesn't need any showy façade for the world, and it took me some time to find the corroded brass plate set into the ruin of a building that had ferns growing out of the drain pipes. The plate said "Yin Tao and Partners," with underneath in smaller letters, "Importers and Exporters," which is what I label my own business, and it can cover a multitude of commercial sins.

There was a dark passage and then stairs leading up to a clacking typewriter. The girl behind the machine looked like one of the sins, efficient in many directions, and ambitious. All visitors interested her so long as they were male.

"How can I serve you?"

That came straight out of a three-year-old American picture shown at the twice-weekly local Rio Cinema. It was extraordinarily quiet in the building, while the girl waited, with her smile, as though the whole place was a listening ear.

"I've come to see Mr. Yin. Without an appointment, I'm afraid."

"Please excuse me one moment."

The politeness around here was impressive, if little else was. The typewriter qualified as an antique and the desk under it could lose a fight against wood beetle at any moment. The window opened onto one of those Oriental courtyards where the mystery is all dirt. This one had a damp stained wall opposite and when I looked down, a sleeping cat below.

I had met Yin twice on my earlier visits to Bintan, both times in the Residency during the dreadful parties John had to give to local leaders, at which the compulsion to invite and to attend is something totally beyond the inclinations of the people concerned, with a resultant misery to all. Mr. Yin and I had talked for perhaps ten minutes on both occasions, and with the more than slight embarrassment which is inevitable between a man who is Mr. Yin's five-feet-two and another going up to about a foot nearer heaven. The problem, which is recurrent with me, had been how to stand, whether by shoving out my legs in a kind of splits I could avoid peering down. But the peering down had been inevitable and resented by someone who kept in mind all the time that many of history's best brains have come in small packages. I'm quite willing to grant this, only qualifying it with the reminder that there have been some quite intelligent big fellows around, too.

Mr. Yin, I remembered, had brought the wisdom of old China up to date with a cynicism he didn't always manage to keep urbane. In fact he was a nasty little tyke.

The inner door opened.

"Mr. Yin is willing to see you," the career girl said. Which was gracious of him.

The inner office continued that contempt for success backgrounds, the too small desk strewn with debris it was inconceivable could still be important to its user. The air was on the heavy side from cheroot smoke which hadn't escaped through half-closed shutters and there was a fifteen-candlepower bulb burning. The general effect in there was of an intense clutter of the kind usually only achieved by highly imaginative television designers. It was too cute to be real.

Mr. Yin, however, was not. He didn't rise to greet me. The bulb hung almost between us, but not strong enough to dazzle. We looked at each other for seconds and an earlier lack of mutual warmth was restored. He started things with a few words not unmarked by pomp.

"It is good of you to call on me when you have such a short time only in Bintan." A pause. "I had heard from Mr. Gissing that you were coming to escort Miss Harpen away from a place of tragedy. Won't you sit down?"

There was a chair without folders on it. I pulled this a little forward, at the same time pushing shut the door which hadn't clicked behind the girl.

"You will be grieved for your friend," Mr. Yin told me.

"And you aren't?"

He looked puzzled.

"I don't understand? I had dealings with the Resident, of course, from time to time. But a friend? Not really."

"Very honest of you, Mr. Yin."

"There is no point in not being."

"And yet I had the impression that John saw a lot of you. As a leader of the community here. Private meetings."

"Private? Again I don't understand?"

"In his study. In the late evening."

Yin took his time then, carefully lighting another cheroot. I wasn't offered one.

"Mr. Harris, all this almost suggests an interrogation."

"Do you object?"

"I find it astonishing. And talk of private meetings. I don't know what you're referring to."

"John saw certain people quite often in his study in the late evening. They came quietly through the back courtyard and weren't announced. They weren't seen by anyone. The times when the Resident was available in this way were known."

"I am completely astonished!"

"So you knew nothing about it?"

"Nothing."

"Or that the Sultan saw John this way? Quite often? He used to walk over from the palace without a guard."

"I have only your word for it that His Highness did this. It sounds most unlike him."

"The Sultan used to come all right. I know. I went along one night when I was staying in the Residency to dig John out for a nightcap. He had forgotten to lock the door to the house. The Sultan was with him. Rather an awkward moment for me."

"I can believe it, Mr. Harris. And the Resident explained his little evening sessions to you then, did he?"

"Yes. He said he only functioned efficiently in Bintan by keeping in touch below the level of official contact. He told me the people he saw. Or some of them. Your name was on the list."

John, of course, had given me no names at all. As though he knew this perfectly well Yin smiled, stretching his lips but showing no teeth.

"How curious. Because I have never availed myself of this opportunity. It might have been most useful for Chinese interests in Bintan had I known of it. Perhaps the Resident had intended to let me into these secret councils but never quite got around to it?"

"He got around to it all right."

"Are you saying I'm lying, Mr. Harris?"

"Yes."

"So you're suggesting that I used to go frequently to the Residency in this manner, by a back door and late at night?"

"You went sometimes. Whether frequently or not I don't know."

"In view of the way in which His Excellency met his death would you be prepared to make these allegations in the presence of my solicitor?"

"No. But you can use the tape you've taken of this talk in any way you like."

"I see. Just what is your purpose in coming to see me like this, Mr. Harris?"

"I believe you can help me to find John's murderer."

I was watching him then. He returned to the stretched smile, quite slowly, in his own time.

"Shock tactics," he said. "Most effective. Poor Chinese merchant quivers before sudden sharp attack from man of action."

"Laugh your head off."

"Later, perhaps I will. Now I think I'll just ask you to go, please."

"It's very unlike a Chinese to dismiss a man without first trying to find out all he knows."

"Ah. I'm being lured with new bait. But you are angling in part of stream where fish are well fed. And not hungry. I don't look at your hook at all."

"Even Swiss francs don't interest you?"

"Swiss francs?" There wasn't even polite curiosity in his voice.

"What you were paid three months ago for the Hok Ping rubber estates here in Bintan, of which you held eighty per cent of the shares. They represent your major immovable asset in these parts. They were earning fourteen and a half per cent. Which isn't the kind of investment I get rid of, and certainly not at a cut price."

Mr. Yin's eyebrows went up. It was the first time he had used that trick.

"Cut price?"

"You took a lower price by almost a fifth from a consortium who would pay you in the European currency. And yet the Malay dollar is quite sound."

"Perhaps I wanted Swiss francs for another operation which demanded them."

"Or for the good old Chinese insurance policy placed in the West when the local scene suggests big trouble soon."

"Your deductions are very wild, Mr. Harris."

"Like life out here. Wild and raw. And now there is nothing to keep you in Bintan, Mr. Yin. You have removed your assets and could live anywhere if the situation became unfavorable here."

"Are your agents for information very expensive? I must employ them. But what provoked all this interest in me?"

[90]

"What John didn't say when I mentioned your name back in Kuala Lumpur."

"I must have made quite an impression on you in our two earlier meetings, Mr. Harris."

"You did."

"I'm gratified. Would you enjoy a cup of green tea? Miss Ching nearly always has some ready."

I didn't stay for tea.

The hire car was waiting for me outside. I got in, gave an address, and sat back to stare at nothing. Whatever Yin might think of my policy it can be a sound tactic to shock the enemy with a full statement of what you know. It is quite likely to precipitate panic action, and that is always less effective than action which has been planned for a long time, and with deliberate care. It all hangs, of course, on being sure that you have located your enemy. I was only fairly sure.

The State Treasurer of Bintan was also the local collector of taxes, another man I had met at John's parties, and left things at that. He had his own offices in the town to keep finance uncorrupted by the rest of the administration. These were spacious, high-ceilinged, and with a faint smell of antiseptic in the fan-stirred air, with the outer defenses guarded by a mature Eurasian woman who looked as though she had decided easy money was more important than love and had then stuck by this philosophy. She was now important and wanted me to know it.

"The State Treasurer never sees anyone without an appointment."

"Naturally not. But I hoped he would make an exception in my case. I have such a short time in Bintan."

"You mean you are leaving by the afternoon boat, Mr. Harris?"

Everyone wanted me on that boat.

"It depends on whether I complete my business."

"In that case, of course . . . Just one moment."

D. P. Hastings, Esq., had carried the civil service trick of never using a Christian name to the point of losing his altogether somewhere about the age of twelve. He'd lost youth soon after that, too. I knew he was a bachelor and scarcely much of a social asset to the local wild set who beat it up with bi-monthly dinner parties in each other's houses. If conversation was forced on the Treasurer he made an effort to respond, but the man was sadly lacking in small talk. He was compact and gray and trim except for his eyebrows which defied the rest of his personality and sent out tough, unruly sprouts of growth.

I didn't know how Hastings had got on with John and in our inevitable references to the Resident's death he gave me no clue. The almost reptilian stillness of the man was a little unnerving. He sat hunched into himself, motionless to the point where I found myself half expecting to see suddenly a long forked tongue come shooting out over white blotting paper. His eyes stayed focused on my face in a glazed but wary attentiveness and my questions faintly alarmed him at first. The small dragon guarding Bintan's treasure didn't like nosy strangers.

Charm was no use; I had to suggest a threat to Bintan's economic self-sufficiency. That made him blink. And talk.

"I don't see what you're getting at, Mr. Harris."

"Chinese money is leaving here. A lot of it."

He blinked again.

"Even if that should be the case, our economy is based on oil revenues."

"I know. But in a very short time everything except oil revenues will be controlled from Singapore. And this realizing of local assets here seems to have happened in an odd rush recently. In a matter of weeks. Did John know about all this?"

"I have no idea."

"You never discussed the matter?"

"Never. Further, I'm sure he would have approved. We were in disagreement on the point of increasing ties with the Federation of Malaysia. The Resident favored it."

"But you don't?"

"That is correct. Chinese money can leave if it likes. Our position is happy without their investment."

"Perhaps, if you know, you'll tell me how much Chinese money, roughly, has gone out?"

"No, sir, I will not!"

"I take it you mean a great deal?"

"You can take what you like, Mr. Harris. I've said nothing."

He was wrong there, he'd said a lot.

I walked from the Treasury to the post office, along Bintan's main street which an easing of the heat had half filled with shoppers, mostly women out looking for afternoon bargains and carrying huge handwoven baskets in which to take these home. Everything seemed as I remembered it except the local near-approach to a department store, Chinese-owned, which had shutters up over its three plate-glass windows and a sign saying closed for alterations.

The post office had been built in 1884 during a phase of great enthusiasm for the durability of colonialism. It was stone, with massive arches upstairs and down, and out in front an arc of chained-off grass on which sat a bronze statue of Sir Wilton Massingham, the first Resident, wearing the kind of clothes for the tropics which had almost certainly accelerated his early death in office. So many of these memorials have been melted down in recent years that it was rather heartening to see Sir Wilton still holding his own, if generally unnoticed.

I read the Latin motto over the main doors, something about easy communications being the key to civilization, an illusion which didn't save Rome or the British Empire, and then went in to a tiled coolness where two clerks took turns to stay awake. It wasn't necessary to disturb either of them. I only wanted the one public telephone box I'd discovered in the state.

Ursula answered the ringing herself. She sounded perturbed. Everyone, including Charlie, had been quite frantic about what had happened to me. Where on earth had I gone? I didn't tell her a picnic.

"Charles has been at the rest house twice. All they could tell him was that you'd gone off in a hired car. What have you been doing?"

"Seeing local businessmen. It's something I never neglect wherever I go. You can make some surprise sales by the personal-contact approach."

"Sales?" Ursula sounded astonished.

"Basically I'm a salesman."

"Really?"

She considered that and I could practically hear my social rating slipping a few notches.

"Charles wants to see you, I think. Can you come here now?"

"Where is he?"

"At the palace again."

"In that case we'd better make it this evening. I rang up to ask about Lil."

"Well, she hasn't come out of her room. I was up again about twenty minutes ago, but she just told me to go away, that there was nothing she wanted. She hasn't eaten anything."

"I shouldn't think that will hurt her."

"You weren't still hoping to get her on today's boat?"

"No, it's pretty close to sailing time. We'd better make it tomorrow. I'll get in to see her tonight."

"Poor Shah Valli. Wasn't it dreadful? Charles is going to be worried about you wandering around in the town after what happened."

Somehow I didn't think Charles would be worrying about me at all.

Clement P. Winburgh was an American newsman on holiday from Vietnam and from telling his readers back home they were in for a twenty years' war. He had arrived by the boat from Latuan, started sightseeing at once—which included color pictures of the Sultan's palace—and as a result of all this tourism was now sprawled on the rest house veranda with a drink in his hand, his suitcases arranged about him. It was encouraging that the bar service had started up again.

I was greeted with a lifted glass.

"Hiya. They told me the local Hilton was crowded out with another guest. You must be it."

He was on the short side, his hair cropped for travel with the Army in helicopters. He had wide blue eyes which had started out finding life wholly good but now wondered. He was happily empty of solutions for the problems in which he had been wallowing and instead of being informative began to ask questions at once, which is good for the ego of a new acquaintance. Every now and then you meet someone like this whom you know at once you'll want to meet again and it helps sustain the tired heart. I had been beginning to feel the lack of team support in this place from Harris and Company personnel and Clem was a godsend to me.

It was a while before I could get him to talk about himself. He had given up newspapers for national magazines which he said were turning to the kind of journalism that suited him, stark realism. He didn't know how long the magazines were going to be able to carry on with this approach and avoid bankruptcy but meantime they paid him well. Like so many in the business he had been married once but wasn't now. He was fair to his ex-wife, marveling that she had hung on for so long.

"This is all right," Clem said, stretching out his legs. "Over

there just across water you sit out on the veranda and somebody lobs in a plastic bomb."

"You been upstairs yet?"

"No, why?"

"They've tidied up, but there still aren't any banisters."

The facts brought a jumpy look into his eyes.

"Friend, next time I want a holiday I'm taking it in
Hawaii. Who hates you? Don't tell me it's not political.
Everything's political. But I only came here for the swim-
ming."

"Move down a few feet. Out of the target area."

"Oh, Lord! I was told this is the one place in Southeast
Asia where nothing ever happens."

"No tourist company out here can really keep up to date
these days. And you'd have been all right for two weeks ending after breakfast this morning."

"What the hell's happening now?"

"I'm busy trying to find out. Clem, have you ever arrived in
a nice peaceful-looking town where, in spite of appearances,
you could already smell tomorrow's violence?"

"Are you one of those psychic nuts?"

"No. My nose is my guide. You'll have a ringside seat when
this little country makes its surprise bid to catch up with contemporary history."

"Has that boat I came on sailed back?"

"Yes. Let me get you another drink."

We ate together in a too-bright dining room where the
moths came in to batter at the lamps and the too-wide windows were open onto a black night. By that time Clem knew
something of my suspicions.

"I'm old enough not to want a scoop," he said. "If there's
going to be some kind of blow-up here I'm just not looking at
it. And anyway the British Empire isn't in my field of authority. I once had three days in Singapore and at the end of it I

said, boy, there's a real problem here and I'm glad it's **not** mine."

"Singapore isn't British Empire now."

"Sure, sure, say it. What were all those big white men with plenty wampum doing around the place?"

I explained carefully that if you get out of an empire at the right time you can leave the whole atmosphere permeated with a good will which your businessmen can use. He listened, chewing, then said:

"Fellow, it's not working in Africa."

"We're thankful for small mercies. It's working in India and places out here."

"And this is where your stake is, eh?"

"I'm a Malaysian citizen."

He looked at me. Then he reached across the table to shake my hand.

"I never met a hundred per cent Oriental with your eye shape before, but here's a firm clasp to East-West friendship. And call on me anytime for a big-dollar loan."

It had taken me a remarkably short time to learn to love this man. We were smoking U.S. cigars when car headlights brightened up black Borneo and then swung in toward the rest house. We sat listening to feet on the veranda, then feet in the lobby and finally feet coming toward the table from a door which had my back to it.

"Paul!"

Charlie Gissing was facing a crisis. It was all over his face and reached down into his hands.

"Have some coffee?"

"No! Why didn't you come to the Residency? Lil's disappeared."

I took a deep breath, from guilt.

"Since when?"

"We don't know exactly. Ursula talked to her about four.

[97]

Lil said she wanted to sleep and wouldn't have dinner."

"Where have you looked?"

"The Residency. And the grounds. Not a sign of her."

"Did she take anything with her?"

"Ursula's not sure. We don't quite know what she had. Paul, where can she have gone in this town? She doesn't know anyone."

"Would there have been time after Ursula spoke to her to get on that boat back to Latuan? It sails at four-thirty, doesn't it?"

"Yes. But she couldn't have made it unless she took a taxi. All the cars are in the garage."

"She could have met a taxi outside the gates. Is there a phone in her room?"

"No. The upper hall landing is the nearest."

I got up.

"Excuse us, Clem."

"Carry right on. Any emergency around here finds me a complete passive resister. But if you do get back tonight look in for a bourbon."

SIX

I WENT out with Charlie to his car.

"What about the police?" I asked. "Have you rung Manson?"

"No. I left that to you."

"I suppose we should remember that Lil knows her way about Bintan. And probably a lot of people here as well."

"What makes you say that?" Charlie's voice had a snap in it. "She was only out on holidays. And as a child never went into town without Shah Valli or someone. She doesn't know a lot of people at all. There isn't any obvious place she could go. We've phoned all the possibles, including the oil company compound. They haven't seen her since she arrived with John. As a matter of fact I think we're the only ones she has seen, except the police at the time of the murder."

He made a noisy gear change.

"Paul, both Ursula and I wish you'd just collected the girl and caught today's boat. Which is what we thought you were going to do. I have enough on my plate just now without this happening."

"Trouble?"

"There's always trouble in this job."

"It's extraordinary how everyone wants me out of Bintan. Or neutralized in it."

"What are you talking about?"

"Linau offered to adopt me this afternoon."

The car wobbled.

"Eh?"

"She wanted to take me home and keep me safe. Guaranteed protection against another attempt on my life, with all home comforts thrown in."

After a moment he said:

"That woman's a law unto herself. Always has been."

He had a reason not to like Linau, maybe more than one. And the state of his nerves wasn't totally accounted for by Lil's disappearance.

Ursula, on the other hand, had returned to an impregnable composure and been efficient. She gave me a decent whisky in the canna-lily room and stated that she had phoned the offices of the Latuan-Bintan steamship company who had assured her there was no question of Lil being on board when the ship went in the afternoon. The traffic had been light, only seven people for Latuan, all of them known.

Which meant that the girl was still somewhere in Borneo, that large island. I was worried, but not to any point of panic. Lil had given a very strong impression of being able to look after herself in a way, and Bintan harbors no organized crime at all, no hint of a white-slave traffic and not much routine wickedness beyond cockfighting. If you want to stray from your wife you go along to the nearest divorcée who has set up as a man-comforter in her own straw-roofed shack. The streets of the town and outlying roads after dark are a lot safer than London or New York. An occasional panther does come down from the hills, but these usually only take dogs.

The police headquarters switched me through to the chief's bungalow and Manson came to the phone sounding like a man talking through food in his mouth which he hoped he'd be allowed to digest in peace.

"Really searched the place, have they? She isn't hiding in a broom cupboard?"

"I'm told not."

"In that case I'll get out the patrol cars."

"How many have you got?"

"Two. Quite enough for our normal needs. We don't have kidnappings."

"That's what I thought."

"Probably find she couldn't bear the thought of eating another Residency meal and is now tucking into duck and mushrooms at Wong Kee's. We'll check. Having a bit of trouble with your ward, aren't you?"

"How did you know?"

"I know all the unimportant things. Ring you back in an hour or so. Will you be staying at the Residency?"

"Yes."

"I'll be in touch. And don't worry about the girl being found hanging from a tree: Suicide doesn't run in the family."

I went upstairs to have a look at a now-unlocked bedroom. It seemed ready to receive Lil again and she had certainly been thinking about what to wear, trying out several sets of shirts and trousers, leaving the ones vetoed on the floor. No one had been allowed in to tidy up.

I flicked on the record player and at once heard Boots and his Bangers.

> I got what you ne—ee—eed,
> You got what I wa—aa—ant . . .

It was a noise to make you glad you'd got a lot of your life over before this happened. Here I could stop it.

The bathroom had a w.c. with "Shanks, Improved Climax 1907" printed on it and a washbasin by the same makers, but progress hadn't got beyond this; the bath was a huge jar of brown porcelain from which you dippered out water to pour over your body, standing on wooden slats above zinc-covered drainage to do it. There were still puddles of water down there and one of the big towels was damp. The girl had planned to go somewhere, freshening-up before she did. No snatch was indicated and a string with nylon briefs on it suggested it hadn't been her intention to clear out for good.

I've never been trained to look for clues and anyway the police wouldn't want me messing things up, so I pottered. A carpenter had built in shelves beyond the Victorian wardrobe and Lil's treasures were arranged there in the open plan, not too tidily either. The few books were leftovers from childhood with only a couple of recent additions to suggest a deepening of literary taste, *Goldfinger* and *Dr. No.* There was also a fat pile of magazines of the only kind it is really economic to publish these days, about half of them with the Bangers leering from splash covers. Then I picked up a real relic.

This was a photograph album. It was something for which I was directly responsible, though I had forgotten. When she was ten I gave Lil a camera and presumably this album. On the first page she had identified herself:

Lil Harpen,
  The Residency,
    Bintan,
      Borneo,
        The World,
          Inner Space.

Facing this I had received the honor of the first portrait. I've never photographed well and Lil's total innocence of technique hadn't worked to my advantage. I looked distressingly smug and overdressed for a holiday, posed against one of those terrible clumps of pampas grass out front. I turned the page and got a jolt. The second picture was of my wife, also with grass. I haven't kept photos of her, I don't think they do any good. Underneath, in spidery writing, was "Aunty Ruth" followed by a later and simple obituary notice . . . "Dead now." The space opposite, perhaps in tribute, had been kept blank. I turned another page.

Lil had apparently used up her first spool on a day her

father gave one of his long-ago parties, catching the guests as they arrived, and making some of them stand, as she had my wife and me, for semiformal portraits. There was the Sultan, already very fat, and with a portion of his Rolls showing, smiling for the little girl it was policy to please. He was in a turban with a plume attached and the jeweled "Star of Borneo" pinned where chest became stomach, just above the cummerbund. Lil had given el Badas a status to which he was scarcely entitled, calling him "His Imperial Highness, the Sultan of Bintan."

Opposite a picture had been torn out. Only the writing remained. "Her Imperial Highness, the Princess Linau." I went on turning over. The book contained the result of twelve experiments, a full spool, no more, most of them blurred, but all inserted. Only Linau had gone, taking bits of the black page facing with her.

"Found anything?" Charlie asked from the doorway.

I closed the album.

"No."

"We've been telephoning around some more. To people she just might have known."

"Negative?"

"Yes."

I was somehow certain the police report would be negative, too. I was thinking of a kid taking photographs, and of change.

Clem was under his mosquito net. He had the bourbon with him, but shoved it out.

"I've been reading in here. Found the book downstairs. *History of Sarawak.* Great stuff, white raja. Why isn't it a movie?"

"It has been."

"This raja?"

"Near enough."

"Quite a guy. Did they find the girl?"

"No."

The net fluttered and Clem emerged. He was wearing pajama bottoms and had the neat look of an all-American father about to be photographed in the bathroom with two all-American children for a toothpaste commercial.

"What's going on?"

"I don't really know."

"So you're being calm about it?"

"The alternative is to tear chunks out of my hair and wail that I've failed in my duty. Which I have."

Clem lit a cigarette and stood brooding.

"Lil Harpen? I think I must have read about her in a news magazine. But Stateside scandals seem kind of remote when you're sitting in an undermanned strong point waiting for the Viet Cong. You have a selection of the much maligned younger generation around you and I found that my main idea was seeing that they all got home in one piece. Even if they don't turn out any outstanding models of rectitude when they get there. I'm sorry for those boys, Paul, plenty. Ever fought in a war you couldn't win?"

I had, but I shook my head.

"There's a permanent contraction in the lower part of your stomach. And you just hate politicians. You really just hate them."

He whacked a mosquito.

"Those boys have more guts than I ever had. They go on battering a soft rubber ball, which gives and pops out again. I should have been a preacher. I've got the gift. What's the matter with your Lil? She been sleeping around?"

"Not exactly around."

"Look, friend, I've lost my halo. Occupational risk. You still got yours?"

"Clem, she's eighteen and she's taken up with a jumping, bawling runt."

"Maybe she'll know better next time. You don't think her

boy friend could have sneaked quietly into this country and she's tucked up with him somewhere?"

"No."

"Then maybe she's dug up a raja she used to know. I'm told a lot of them are good-looking."

"I don't think that's it."

"You're beginning to look like daddy. It puts years on you. Have another drink."

I sat down and Clem went back in behind the mosquito curtains. I asked him how close he thought we had become in six hours.

"Just like roommates at college," he said. "Why?"

"I need your help."

"That's different. I've lost touch with all my old roommates. You write at Christmas and then that stops. I've never been one for class reunions, either. And as I pointed out earlier, I'm on holiday. Whatever is wrong around here can stay wrong with no American aid forthcoming."

"I was followed back here," I said.

Clem pushed out of the net.

"You're a disturbing contact, Paul. I'm tired of climbing in and out of this damn thing. So you were followed back?"

"I want to go out again, and with no followers."

"To look for the girl?"

"Not directly."

"What is this?"

When I didn't make any statement he switched on his neat little transistor, fiddling for the American forces relay from Okinawa, but first we got Radio Bintan, with *Ronggeng* music.

"Hold it," I said.

"You like this stuff?"

"It ought to be about their signing-off hour. I want to check that Bintan is being put to sleep for the night."

In about five minutes we got that, another tropic day over,

and nothing left but sweet dreams in your attap-roofed hut unless you had any private plans. I sat there thinking about Radio Bintan.

It was one of the Sultan's personal projects for progress from which he got what advertising revenue there was, not much. But it was also the communications network with the outside world, something el Badas took over when the cable company closed down its local office. It was interesting, when you thought about it, that all communications in and out of the country, all legal ones that is, passed through the palace, except the telephone. And even here if you phoned in a telegram for Singapore or London the message was radioed from the palace, too, which is a useful kind of control to have in a benevolent despotism. The Residency had their own in-and-out set, of course, for coded contact with the Colonial Office, but it seemed highly probable that el Badas wouldn't be one to grant licenses to radio hams. The local big daddy liked to keep everything under his hand and it would be quite possible for the Sultan to seal off his little country at any time just about as effectively as the bosses of Peking-orientated Albania manage to do. On consideration I didn't like this situation much.

Another thing I didn't like was no phone call from Ohashi. I'd asked Lee Wat about any calls for me and been told none had come in. But when my assistant says he'll do something he does it. I've never known him to forget.

"You look like the last of the British raj in a 'B' movie," Clem said. "And there's no more bourbon."

"Would you mind sleeping in my bed for a couple of hours?"

He stared.

"What? Is another assassination attempt that imminent?"

"No. I've searched my room. It's okay. I think the orders are to leave me alone tonight, so long as I stay put. All I want you to do is cross over the hall without being seen in a

[106]

few minutes, then lock the door and put out the light. After a bit you snore."

"I don't snore."

"I do. And the people covering me just might know that."

"I've always been a man to rush like a lemming into the wrong situations. I like my own bed."

"Clem, I've got to get out of here unseen. It's important."

"So's my life to me. And your personal magnetism just isn't strong enough to turn me into a willing stooge."

He sat down suddenly.

"Just what is all this, Paul?"

"Trouble."

"You think it's the Red bogey again, don't you? Right here in quiet little oil-rich Bintan?"

"Yes."

"That ought to make me leap up like a brass band had started the Star-Spangled Banner. But if you stay in these parts for long enough you get a kind of moral rheumatism. I don't jump to attention any more. I've got too many aches for a smart reaction."

"I'm only asking you to go to bed."

"The wrong bed. Do you know what I've been dreaming about lately? Becoming the star reporter on a small-town newspaper in Idaho. All I want now are the simple things, good climate, good meat, and a lot of mountains all round to keep off the hydrogen blast. I can hear western America singing any time I stop to listen, and it's a beautiful sound."

He went in behind the mosquito curtains.

"What's this great long bolster for? I've never seen anything like it? Takes up a lot of room."

"Colonial invention. For the hated imperialists. Known as a Dutch wife. I was offering you the hospitality of mine."

"Just like an Eskimo chief." He backed out again. "All right, you win. And may my martyred blood be forever on your conscience. This is how the British have got us into all recent wars. By just sitting and looking sad. As though you couldn't really believe your cousins would let you down. It wouldn't be natural."

"That's right," I said.

He went over to the door, opened it, looked carefully up and down out there, then turned his head back to whisper.

"God dammit, how I hate limeys. Even Scotch limeys."

When I was alone I switched on the radio to the Okinawa relay. It's always heartening in Asia to hear American jazz sent out from a loudspeaker more powerful than anything the Chinese have got. The voice which broke in for a news flash was corn-fed in Iowa and hearty, only doing time in the Orient. I heard him out, then cut off the Dixieland.

Clem had been right about the bogey. The thing had been with me for a long time now, getting steadily bigger. After the uncertain factor of Vietnam the only real unit of resistance between two pressure groups is Malaysia, with Mao planning to move south toward it and Indonesia trying hard to walk in without knocking. The little country to which I belong could soon be like Britain in 1940, isolated and very lonely. And Bintan, tiny as it was, represented a chip out of the northern half of this Malaysian geographical boomerang. In the hours since I had landed in it I'd become very conscious of how important the little chip was, and it seemed almost certain to be about to hit tomorrow's headlines.

It was pitch black out on the veranda, no moon at all, with the quilted warmth of a windless tropic night. I went along to the last pillar and leaned over, listening. I didn't hear a thing, even from the kitchens. I went down slowly, getting my legs around the upright, and keeping body weight on my hands until the last minute. The short slide only produced the hiss of my trousers against wood.

Lights were out in the service wing, but I heard voices from one of the detached, two-room staff quarters and there was a soft, rosy glow over there. I found what I wanted propped against a wall, a bicycle fitted with a big carrier over the front wheel.

The Residency was closed down for the night, too, as though the flap over Lil had reached a climax in weariness and suddenly been shut off. I pushed the bike across acres of mown grass, using shrub cover where I could, with no trickle of light from anywhere in that mass bulk ahead of me, then went around to the back of the building, taking the route used by those coming for late-night consultations with John.

It looked as though this tradition was being carried on. Closed shutters filtered light down onto the concrete floor of a shelter veranda outside the study. I couldn't see through the angled slats at all, and the first set of shutters resisted my cautious attempt to pull them back. The second lot moved on oiled hinges, which made me take a slow breath and wait. I heard a match being struck in the room.

Charlie was at the big desk, sitting in John's chair, with an anglepoise lighting up what looked like a huge ledger. He was wearing specs and in the process of lighting a pipe.

"Hello again," I said.

Apparently his visitors normally obliged with a little arrival noise. If it hadn't been a heavy chair Charlie would have knocked the thing over getting out of it. Pipe and glasses fell onto the floor.

"What in hell's name . . . ?"

"Sorry. I should have knocked."

"You! What do you want?"

"A chat. It seemed a good time. I had a feeling you might be up. Though I thought the police had sealed this room off?"

"I . . . I have a key."

If I'd been a doctor I wouldn't have liked Charlie's color. It's a sign of years or general debility when shock takes time to wear off. He went on looking like a man who ought to be settled down somewhere and given a nice restoring cup of tea.

So I was charitable and gave him time to recover, using it to lock the shutters and close glass doors over both sets of windows which meant the temperature would rise, but privacy would be improved.

"Ursula in bed?"

"What business is it of yours?"

"None, but I was hoping we wouldn't be interrupted."

"Yes, she's in bed."

The ledger on the desk had John's writing on the open pages. It was probably a log book of administrative routine, the record of a life set down in paras on items like village sanitation, but with no personal note a biographer could use at all. The assistant could have been poring over his master's notes, trying to use them as a guide to power.

Behind that big chair and taking up about a third of one wall were twin steel doors which opened back to reveal the Residency radio set. The lock was a combination, to cut out any distresses over lost keys.

"Why are you here?"

"I'm restless. Thinking about John's murder. In this room. As a matter of fact I was going to commit a felony and break in. To have a look around. But I see it has been very neatly tidied up."

"The police don't think it was murder!"

"You're wrong, Charles. Manson does. Didn't he tell you?"

"What?"

"Just a private opinion, of course. Even a policeman has them."

"Are you saying that . . . ?"

Charlie was suffering from an inability to finish sentences. He had settled again in the high-backed chair, as though hoping it gave him some authority, which it didn't. I found myself looking down at the plump little man with no love and small charity.

"It interests me, Charles, that murder didn't seem highly probable to you as well."

"I thought about it. We all did. But the reasons for suicide . . ."

"You worked with John for years. You really believe he could have killed himself?"

"How do we know what makes people do things? How can we know?"

"We can try to find out. When we're involved personally."

"I'm not the police!"

"You were supposed to be a devoted friend."

An odd thing happened. I'd never seen tears just flood into a man's eyes before, but Charlie's were suddenly awash. He put his arms out over the ledger and dropped his head down onto them, his shoulders moving. John's careful records were in danger of being soaked out in saline solution, but I didn't think it was any dodge on Charlie's part to blur what he had been reading. Even a highly trained actor couldn't be expected to have that kind of control over the ducts leading to the eyes.

"Oh, God," he said. "Oh, God in Heaven!"

"Even in our time a few people still believe He's up there. Watching."

"Shut up. Shut up!"

"Charles, whose game are you playing here?"

His head twisted on those stretched-out arms.

"What are you talking about? I don't know . . ."

"I called on Yin Tao this afternoon."

Charlie's head came up then, slowly. The plump don't cry well. His face looked like a balloon on which the color has run.

"Yin Tao? What's he to do with . . . ?"

"I'm asking you."

"What?"

"Why is Yin Tao all packed up and ready to leave Bintan if he has to? The man hasn't got a single asset left here, unless you consider that moldy building from which he operates an asset. And for all I know he may have sold that to the Department of Works. Under a local slum clearance act."

"Yin Tao leaving?"

"I wouldn't say that. Just buying insurance abroad. In case local plans go wrong. They all do it when they can, and trouble is near. Almost a national trait. And, Charles, he laughed at me. Which was a bit of a shock. Because a man like Yin doesn't laugh at the opposition unless he has everything sewn up so tight he's sure nothing can threaten him. I went into that office thinking I represented quite a considerable threat just by my presence in Bintan. But I came out knowing I didn't. Chastening."

"I know nothing about Yin's affairs!"

"So he doesn't come here to give you his orders?"

That brought Charlie up out of the chair and for fleeting seconds I had the feeling he meant to sweep up a long thin paperknife as he straightened. But he was just standing there in a bid for dignity.

"I am the Acting Resident of this state!"

He was pathetic.

"Yes, Charles."

"Yin has never been here to see me. Or . . . anyone."

"All right. But they used to come and see John. The way I came in has been used often before. And one set of shutters were unlocked."

"No one was coming here!" He shouted that.

"No longer any need?"

"What do you mean?"

"Everything's sewn up, isn't it? Everything in this little state. And you know why."

"No!"

"I'd help you."

"Would you? What do you think you could do, Mister Paul Harris?"

"You can always do something when you know all the facts."

"I don't know what you mean when you talk about facts."

"Even when this state is cut off from the outside world, except for your radio?"

That hit him. He stared.

"What makes you think that?"

"A guess. But I'm damn sure that a cable from me to Singapore tonight would never get past the Sultan's palace."

"Nonsense!"

"Let's test things out. I'll put through to Kuala Lumpur long distance on this phone. Any objections?"

"This isn't a call box!"

"There's a great shortage of them in your state."

I put out my hand to the receiver. He called out:

"Leave it alone!"

He swung away and went over to a cupboard where John had kept his drinks, the top half a locked gunrack for sporting rifles, the bottom for bottles. This had been the Resident's real living room. Charles didn't suggest I join him; his whisky was medicinal. He drank it and stood staring at the wall.

"The trouble has nothing to do with Yin. It's the Sultan. He's playing an old game again. Because John's not here, and I am." There was bitterness in that. "He thinks he can just use me. The great el Badas, descendant of pirates, rotten crook."

"A nice summing-up, Charles. Is it oil royalties?"

"Yes. And this time it's not the two or three per cent he'd have asked from John. He wants twenty. That would put him on sixty-forty basis with the oil company. It's crazy and he knows it."

"So your trips to the palace today?"

"Yes."

He went on staring at the wall. Then he needed some more medicine, not a modest prescribed dose, either. I was glad to see a lot of it going in because almost certainly alcohol made Charlie feel so much bigger than he was.

"What's the blackmail against you?" I asked.

The Acting Resident turned.

"Oh, very smart. Something el Badas could never have thought of by himself. Linau put him up to it. That's what she used to do in John's time. Come back from one of her damn trips abroad with something else for her brother to try out. The oil company is there to be squeezed and Linau goes off to think up new ways of doing it. Now it's the really big gamble. If el Badas doesn't get that twenty per cent additional cut for himself and his tribe of relations he's going to revoke the concession given by his late uncle on the grounds that it had been misrepresentation to the old man. He threatened me with a declaration of independence from British protection."

I knew I was now in acute danger of losing American aid in the person of Clem. You simply can't ask a United States citizen to take action against someone else's declaration of independence, especially when this involves standing shoulder to shoulder with the British, or even the ex-British. That tea party in Boston at once blurs the issue with strong sentiment. Not to mention the follow-up War of 1812.

The Sultan had hit on something effective this time: the lion's share of the oil take or a withdrawal from the Empire. Just like that. There seemed to me, however, certain holes in his instrument of blackmail.

"Have you asked for British troops to be flown in here?"

Charlie shook his head.

"No. El Badas says if I do it he'll deny having raised the question of royalties at all—that I misunderstood him. Which will make me look a bigger fool at the Colonial Office than I do already."

His humility, as it always is, was rather touching. But bitterness came into his voice as he went on:

"They'd have believed John. I'm a different proposition. And the Sultan knows this perfectly well. Troops would arrive to find a peaceful, happy little state, no hint of trouble, everyone smiling. His Highness, slightly puzzled, would nonetheless give a cocktail party for the officers of the battalion and offer to lend them polo ponies. Damn him!"

"You're sure no one would listen to you?"

"I wouldn't be given the benefit of the doubt. If there's a mess here London would expect me to be in charge at the time it happened. That's my rating."

"You could still get in first with a full radio report."

"The moment I switch on that set el Badas will know, from his monitors. Code won't help me. He doesn't need to know what I'm saying to guess what it'll be. And that contact with London would be the signal for sweetness and light in Bintan."

"Have you the power to deal with the oil company for el Badas?"

"No, of course not. But I make the claim official the moment I take it up. London is then committed to some action. And that's all that el Badas wants from me. He doesn't expect twenty per cent, but he hopes in the end to get five."

"You're sure Linau's behind this?"

"Who else? That woman is the empire builder in the family. She knows damn well she'd never have got another penny out of John. He spent all his time trying to use the el Badas cut for state improvements, not their pockets. They were frightened of John."

"And so they killed him?"

"I don't know. I just don't know!"

I went over to the cupboard and poured good whisky into a cut glass.

"What would this declaration of independence really mean, Charles?"

"Well, Bintan would be declared a free state, British protection revoked, and there would be the usual immediate application for a seat in the United Nations."

Before long they were going to need a new building over there in New York.

"Could the Sultan get away with just taking over the oil company? They tried it in Iran and it didn't work."

"It might work here. Things have changed since Iran. What you do now is whip up anticolonial sentiment via the Afro-Asian bloc and while you're doing that appeal for technical help from behind the Iron Curtain. Badas would get it quickly, too. From the Russians. Technicians, everything. It would give them the hold they've been looking for in these parts. A checkmate for Mao. Linau could have carried out all the preliminary negotiations. She's just back from Hong Kong. You can meet anyone you want in Hong Kong, from anywhere."

"It couldn't be Yin pushing el Badas?"

"You've got Yin on the brain, Paul! I don't know why you're dragging him into this. He's just small business these days, that's all."

Small business since the oil company started up, and not liking the role.

"Has el Badas given you any time?"

"Twenty-four hours."

"You either put forward his claims by then or Bintan goes independent?"

"So he says."

"I'd get on the blower to London."

"The decision isn't yours."

"Do you mind telling me whether you've made it?"

"Yes. I'm not getting in touch with London. I can handle this alone."

For a moment or two I was startled, until it dawned that Charlie wasn't the one who thought he could handle this alone, it was Ursula. She was the Acting Resident's Linau, and his backbone. A regular war of women through proxies, interesting to watch in other circumstances. There was the very real point, too, that if Charlie, with his wife's assistance, could weather this little crisis he would then be in a position to send in the kind of report to London that would be a surprise for the gray men there around a policy table. It would then be very difficult indeed to pass over such an effective colonial servant as Charlie had suddenly turned out to be when it came to choosing a new Resident.

"I'll call the Sultan's bluff," Charlie said, as much for himself as for me. "I do damn all. Then if he tries anything I'll get onto the officer commanding British forces Sarawak direct and ask for paratroops. They could be here in hours. Long before el Badas could get any effective reaction from his appeal to Russia."

"Have you got the right to appeal direct for British forces from another country?"

"Frankly, I don't know. But I should think yes, in an emergency."

It was good old-fashioned imperialism, particularly interesting because it was of the type that John would never for a moment have dreamed of using. There was a change in Charlie now, as though whisky had made passage for a very tiny Napoleonic complex to work its way to the surface. His eyes still held a gleam from the tears that had been in them, but the misery had quite gone and I was looking at a little man who suddenly had hopes of redeeming a long and gently negative life by a sudden, startling master stroke. To have damaged this green shoot of egotism in any way would have put something else on my conscience.

"I give you a toast, Charles. May the protectorate survive until it is federated into Malaysia and the oil revenues have ceased to flow into el Badas' pocket."

"I'll drink to that, if you'll pour me one."

He took the glass, apparently unconscious of the sweat on his face which was the result of strain, not a stuffy atmosphere.

"It's what John would have done," Charlie said, after a gulp.

"I never knew what John would do. I didn't really ever see him in action. Just heard about it after. He was very fond of you."

Charlie's eyes went wet again.

"Did he ever say that?"

"Yes. Just last month in Kuala Lumpur."

"He wasn't . . . laughing at me?"

"I was never with John when he laughed at anyone."

"No, you're right. He didn't. God, how I've missed him ever since . . ."

"Yes."

Charlie began to talk about John. It appeared to be a relief to him to do this. I was standing where I could see the door, with its large, old-fashioned and now-tarnished brass knob. This began to turn, very slowly, right around, then back again. It seemed that Charlie had locked himself in.

"Charles, could I be a nuisance? Lee Wat's food has gone off. I'm starving."

He was my friend now.

"Good Lord, of course, man. I'll get you something. A sandwich?"

"I could come and help forage?"

But he didn't think this a good idea. There was always the possibility of Ursula on the prowl in curlers—more real than he knew—patroling those long-deserted corridors. Charlie turned the key and went out with the confidence of a man who knows that he is leaving nothing dangerous behind and I didn't even look at John's ledger. I didn't look, either, at the combination lock on those steel doors. Nearly everything in this palace of yesterdays was decaying but that lock was contemporary and to deal with it you'd need an oxyacetylene cutter. There was, however, the gun cupboard. In peaceful, law-abiding Bintan this had received minimum security precautions and all I needed to get the doors open was the blade of that long thin paperknife. Inside were shotguns and an elephant rifle from India days, all near-antiques and a couple perhaps collector's pieces. I found the two short Lee Enfields I remembered, Mark III's, leftovers from some colonial war, but still useful little mechanisms. In a drawer beneath were four boxes of 303 ammo.

I lifted out the boxes first and took them, as silently as possible, through the French windows out into the courtyard where the bicycle was parked. The court seemed quite empty but I did a check to make sure. Then I came back in again for the two guns which got tied onto the cycle frame with string from a desk drawer. The closed gun cabinet showed no signs at all of a forced opening. I took out an Ohashi present from Tokyo, a penknife with two blades, a corkscrew, a fingernail or ear-cleaning spike and a small but highly useful screwdriver. I put the screwdriver to work for about a minute and a half.

John had left behind seven Corona-Coronas and I took the band off one, lighting it with proper respect, for it's an unusual cigar to come on out East where everyone smokes the Philippine leaf. A few draws reminded me that Castro still has a hold on capitalism, as the Scots will on solvency with their national product even if the English go bankrupt. John's whisky was a malt which doesn't want to be diluted by tropic water or any water and sitting in his chair I had a few moments of stolen content made sweeter by trouble on each side of them.

SEVEN

CHARLIE came back still the cheerful, bustling good host, which almost certainly meant he hadn't met up with his wife. The sandwiches looked man-made and it was my day for a lot of deep-freeze ham, an insult to the cigar, but I had to eat it. It was a relief when the Acting Resident was coaxed to share my snack and I didn't have to urge him to bring over the bottle of John's whisky. This visit, which had started out on a note of scarcely concealed resentment from Charlie, was now totally happy and I was beginning to get the feeling that I had come to represent stable and reliable factors in an uncertain world. It would have upset the little man considerably to have seen deeply into my thoughts.

We talked about John again, and into this crept the middle-aged hero-worshipper's inevitable slight resentment at his own long-lasting absorption in another's effective life. It wasn't exactly stated that he had given too much of himself to further his friend's interests but there was just a hint that Charles Gissing could have been someone quite different but for this noble sacrifice. John had needed the right kind of second in command and Charlie had fitted himself into this niche, but not in any self-defense against total responsibility. It was Bintan he loved, and after Bintan John. Ursula didn't come into this, which wasn't a great surprise to me. It is very difficult for any husband to love a wife who holds him to his marital duty by the scruff of his neck. Love isn't then the sentiment involved at all, just a lived with and accepted terror.

I was anxious now to get moving and Charlie insisted on accompanying me to the front door, a point of exit I didn't argue about because I didn't want to draw attention to that loaded bicycle. We walked through the mausoleum, with Charlie's leather soles setting up a clattering of life that distant echoes seemed to mock. Each separate, pendant light showed his face naturally shiny from the warmth of a tropic night, but under this sprinkled damp it was now plumply composed.

"Did you walk here, Paul?"

"Yes," I lied.

"Good Lord."

Walking, in hot countries, is still left to the natives.

"We haven't said a word about Lil," he remembered suddenly.

The matter hadn't been quite out of my mind, but near enough. I felt the guilt, too.

"I don't think anything serious could have happened, do you?"

"Probably not," I agreed.

"She rather likes doing things for effect, you know."

I did know. Charles went on:

"She had a Malay nurse she was very fond of. I thought about that earlier. I believe the old woman moved up to Kumpat, which is just up the river. Lil could have gone there. I'll tell the police to check on this in the morning."

I stopped him switching on the hanging, prismatic portico lamp which would have shown us up clearly from the grounds. We stood in a gloom peopled by ghosts of those who had retired at statutory age to end their days in the English home counties and then, uneasy spirits, had returned to this scene of a long-vanished authority. At least half the hauntings in the Far East are organized by former European residents who simply had to get back to the places where they had meant something, even if obliged to die in order to do it.

[121]

"Charles, what do you bet that the daily boat for Latuan will develop engine trouble tomorrow and not be able to sail?"

"That could happen."

"That and a lot else. You wouldn't know that the phone in the study back there is tapped?"

"It's . . . what?"

I couldn't see his face. That was a pity.

"Bugged," I said. "I wonder when the thing was last serviced? Any idea?"

"No." He whispered that, as though suddenly conscious of ghosts, too.

"I took the bottom plate off. Neat job inside. Highly professional. Plastic bombs and phone tapping. Bintan isn't such a backwater. El Badas is bound to have a few good radio mechanics up at his palace, but this sort of thing suggests real specialization. You don't think some of those technicians from beyond the Iron Curtain could have arrived already?"

"It's impossible!" His voice stayed faint.

"I wish I thought so. One thing is certain, Charles, what we said in there tonight went down on tape. So your strategy with the Sultan is known. If I were you I'd go back into the study, cut phone wires, open the radio safe and scream to London for help. I won't say goodnight. It's no time for sleeping."

I went out into the pitch dark and toward what I was certain waited for me there. The gravel on the drive pinpointed my position in those seconds before I got up onto the grass. It was almost the perfect place and time to get me, with more than an hour in which to organize a neat killing, while Charlie and I chatted and ate ham sandwiches. The only advantage I held was the care taken over the removal of that phone plate, no scraping noises, no slipping of the screwdriver. They hadn't total surprise to use, and this was something.

The Residency was dark again, Charlie hiding in it somewhere, perhaps scared enough now to take the only action that could save him. He'd been given his chance. I was half sorry for the man, but only half. It gives me no pleasure to watch a liar slowly beginning to swell with pride at the sheer virtuosity of his performance, especially when it is likely to be a final performance. I didn't think he had known about the phone tap. And if not he would now be realizing that he hadn't been clever at all, a bad time for the little man.

To get to a cobbled outer courtyard I had to cross drive gravel again. The crunching was hideous, but I made myself walk like a man in no great hurry, his cautions for what is ahead, not at his back. When I got onto the smooth cobbles the crunching behind didn't stop for seconds. It wasn't any echo.

I walked down the middle of that outer court toward the arched lane which led, beyond a picket gate, to the inner enclosure where I had left the bike. The gate had once been painted white and I saw it from about eight feet away, the place where I had to stand for a moment.

I stopped and put my hand down for the latch. Then I kicked back. The contact felt like a man's thigh, and wasn't a packed blow. But it did break the attacker's confidence in total surprise, shattering the tension of his purpose. I heard a grunt, but he was on me before I could turn, the cold heat of a blade getting through shirt to my triceps muscle. I dropped John's knife and aimed low with my left for a Chinese head. Contact this time was more effective, the grunt much louder. I could feel the assassin spinning away from me, the stir of air as he did it. His knife fell on cobbles, a nice sound, what I wanted. He wouldn't have time to reach for a gun.

The body I dropped onto was small, but it didn't go down easily, and low punches were a discomfort until I smothered them with weight and we fell, me with a held cushion. He lay on the cobbles without movement, perhaps winded, but I made sure, lifting a head between my two hands and banging it back onto stone, not too hard, but hard enough. The little man was limp when I rolled off him.

I struck a match to see eyes staring and a mouth open. It was Lee Wat, my host at the rest house.

The chatty innkeeper wasn't at all talkative in his other role as a night killer. There was a loaded Colt in his left trouser pocket and I used this as a persuader, making him push the bicycle. We went back to the rest house in the dark, never using the lamp, and very slowly, with Lee sick twice from the sour stomach of failure. I was patient when this happened, but he wasn't allowed to forget the gun.

I kept expecting him to risk a bullet in the kidneys and make a break for it, especially where the road moved through primary jungle for half a mile and blackness was so thick you could only keep going by the feel of tarmac underfoot, but he stayed with me, perhaps from the apathy of shock. Once I heard a sound like a little whimper which didn't move me to any compassion. I remembered the knife, now left to rust with just a little of my blood on the blade. Bleeding at my shoulder had stopped and all I felt was a stiffness that would work off. The hatred I have for killers in the dark wouldn't work off so easily. It was no effort to keep it warm for what I had to do.

I told him we were going to take the bicycle into the rest house and it needed a couple of prods with the gun to get this home. The man seemed lost to me and to himself. I put a hand on his shoulder, a curious team, beautifully synchronized by a threat of death. Lee carried the bicycle up steps and let tires whisper across the veranda. He got out the doorkey himself, without prompting.

It was an easy push across the pitch-black lobby, but on the stairs up Lee started to pant and heave under his load of small arms and I had to help. We went along to the bathroom and shoved the bike in there, too.

I closed the door, locked it, and put on the light. Lee was watching the gun, not me. In my hands it seemed to fascinate him, as though he felt certain one of the bullets in there was labeled for him. I know the feeling and it does concentrate the attention. When I told him to untie the rifles he seemed most willing to oblige and worked slowly, buying time. It might have occurred to the man that if I was going to kill him there were more convenient places than a bathroom, but cerebration had dulled down. Fear had made his face an odd dirty color.

I took one of the cords from the bike and stood back a bit, still with the gun, making two loops for a quick pull tight. I told Lee to hold out his arms and he did, meekly enough, thrusting them forward with hands limp. I didn't quite see those hands close into fists as he drove them into my stomach, his packed weight behind. I lost the gun as he had meant me to do. He used arms, legs and teeth. I slipped on shiny zinc and went down, but brought him, too, by one ankle. He rolled back from me, jerking his body like a snake held by the tail. He kicked the side of my head. If he had been wearing leather the last round would have been his. As it was I could just see his hands going up to the big brown water jar to pull it over on me. I dragged at his ankle. His hands lost grip on the wet edge of the jar and though it wobbled he hadn't the weight to bring it over. I had the weight for what I had to do.

The water level in the big brown jar was down by a foot and a half before Lee Watt answered my question, not by words, he couldn't use words, but a nod. I had put the question twenty times.

"Are you working for Yin Tao?"

We were both soaked. I began to pull away the two gags,

[125]

one on each side of his mouth, rammed into his cheeks, but space for the water to go down his throat. At once he rolled over to lie on his stomach, face downward on the zinc, shuddering spasms pumping water out of his stomach. Then for a while he lay quite still, bound arms behind him, bound feet tight together.

I stood up, dripping. Lee heard the movement and pulled up his knees into the fetal position of withdrawal. He looked dreadfully like a child and he began to cry, very softly, a sniveling despair. There was a voice somewhere, which sounded like my own, shouting at me.

The knife is clean and so is the bullet. What I had done is filthy, the enemy's final weapon which has to be ours, too, if we are to survive. There is no hope of co-existence out where I live. It is going to be one long fight, or perpetual readiness to fight. There are no political solutions with an enemy who laughs at them.

A sound made me look at the door. The handle was moving. I reached for the dipper, filled it, and splashed water again. I couldn't produce the humming of a man taking a bath, but I made enough noise to cover Lee's sounds, which weren't loud. Moments later I went over to the door, gun in hand, with the bicycle torch.

The long straight corridor was empty, nicely tidied up from bomb blast. I locked us in again and took the cords off Lee's feet, propping him up against the pedestal. He wasn't, in those moments, able to look at me, and he didn't try, head slumped down on his chest. I felt a neutral compassion, not for the killer who had tracked me on a black night carrying a gun and a kitchen knife, but for a man who was also something else in his own right, something I had taken from him. I whispered:

"Listen to me. I'm going to let you go. But if you try to warn Yin Tao he'll have you killed. At once. You know that. If you just disappear he'll think I've dealt with you. You have a wife here, don't you? Take her and get out. Right away from the town. Some village up-country might be safe. Or even the jungle. Hide for the next week or so. Think of your wife and hide. They would deal with her, too."

A word shaped on his lips but didn't come. I had a feeling it was another attempt at defiance, stillborn. Then he looked at me. I wasn't getting any thanks for this mercy, he knew it for what it was. How could I keep a prisoner in the rest house? And yet I was giving him back his life. It was something that would not now be offered from his own side. With them failure couldn't be explained away.

I put the Colt in my pocket, took the carrier off the bike, tucked the two Lee Enfields under one arm and went out, leaving Lee Wat in the dark to re-think his future. The passage was very black, with only a faint lightening by the shattered door to what had been my first room. Outside the new one I unloaded carefully and listened, opening the door even more carefully and listening again. There was no sound of breathing from the bed and I brought in my gear, groping about for a stout Victorian wardrobe from which projected a key. This took the guns and ammo nicely, with no clinking while they were stowed away. I locked them up and put the key up into the dust behind a carved pediment.

The room's lighting was one bulb hanging centrally, a moth-attracter with a tin shade which left everything important in half-shadow, bed, washstand, suitcases. I found that Clem had gone back to his own bolster.

I got half an hour lying on that bed, but I didn't sleep. I haven't the gift, so essential in military commanders, of being able to just drop off when the chance presents itself, and waking totally refreshed to issue a crisis order that ten thousand men have to dig in and hold a fixed line at all cost. In my time I've been on the receiving end of a few orders of this kind from cat nappers and never really felt that these commands had been thought through. My crisis situations keep me awake and I just stay awake until they are resolved or I

[127]

flake out. So far I haven't gone into any comas of fatigue fatal to my interests, but it could happen at any time. I believe it was the thought of Lee Wat which made me push my feet out onto the floor and move off out into the passage, wearing only the bottom half of my pajamas. I checked the bathroom to find it empty and the bicycle gone.

Downstairs, even in the dark, the rest house had the feel of a place which has been abandoned. I was pretty certain that a check of the servants' quarters would show all the occupants gone from those little houses, not just Lee and his wife. Bintan was closing down for tourism and a lot of other things.

The phone wire was still alive. A crackling went on for a long time before the buzzer started and that lasted for all of two minutes until broken by a peevish girl's voice demanding, in Cantonese, my business. The switch to English took a moment or two and didn't end in any graciousness achieved.

"What you want?"

"To speak to the manager of the oil company."

"Eh?"

I repeated my request and was told that the manager would be asleep. I asked her just to ring his number and leave the responsibility for waking him to me.

"No."

I hadn't expected quite such a flat refusal.

"You mean you won't put a call through?"

"Cannot. Line down."

"How long has it been down?"

"This night."

"So there is no way of getting through to the oil company?"

"Tomorrow maybe, tonight no."

That was that. It's always unpleasant to have your worst fears confirmed. I went up the stairs again, careful with bare feet about wood splinters that might have escaped an afternoon clean-up.

Clem's door was unlocked. I moved gently enough but he might have been waiting.

"I keep my wallet under my pillow. And to whom it may concern I was a judo black belt at college."

"It's only me."

"Did you say only?"

"Sorry to wake you."

"Sleep isn't one of the things that Bintan offers. I've been lying here with the feeling that sleep and I aren't ever going to come to a decent arrangement again. Have a nice solo out in the black night?"

"Interesting."

"I suppose that's what the professional killer says when he gets home to his wife. Did you kill anybody?"

"No."

"Not even the guest you had in the bathroom?"

"Why not knock and ask in?"

"You might have been with a girl."

"I was with Lee Wat. He tried to knife me at the Residency."

"Oh." There was a pause. "Why bring him here after?"

"I needed water."

Clem took a moment to think about that.

"Paul, it's my feeling you're a rough man. They have to be tolerated in war. But no one has as yet convinced me that this is a war situation."

"Then let me try. There is no communication now in or out of Bintan. It's impossible to phone the oil company. That means a fast-flowing stream between us and the communication resources of that place. I tried to phone just now. The line's down."

"Mightn't that be fairly normal in this community?"

"Yes, it could be. And that's part of the trouble. No communication with the town wouldn't upset them down there too much. They only need the town for vegetables and as a place to take visiting friends. Company policy is to keep smiling and to take no apparent interest in local politics or much else."

"That's never been Harris and Company policy, has it?"

I sat down in the dark.

"Clem, did you go on with that book about Raja Brooke down in Sarawak?"

"What else had I to do? Entertainment for tourists is at an international minimum."

"Then you probably got to the place where the raja, long after he thought the country beautifully pacified, suddenly had a revolution on his hands. Chinese miners from up-country. They swept down on Kuching and damn nearly took over."

"That would be swell in the movie. White raja escapes from fort in nightshirt. To rally his pirates."

"And mop up the Chinese. Nice job they made of it, too, the raja and his Dyaks. Rough on the Chinese. But the point of that story to me seems awfully vivid tonight. Because even a hundred years ago the Chinese were already regarding Borneo as one of their outposts. In which they had special rights. I don't think they've ever forgotten. And that they mean to lay claim to those rights again in the next twenty-four hours."

"You mean in Bintan?"

"Yes."

"Well, you certainly have a sensational proposition here. It will make nice world headlines. That is, after the news commentators have carefully explained to everyone just where Bintan is, and why it is so extremely important and one thing and another. It's my bet that any developments here will catch the commentators on the hop on this little issue. After all, I've been living just across the water and news about Bintan wouldn't have excited me much."

"Bintan will be on the world map soon enough."

[130]

"Unless you can contrive to defeat Chinese machinations singlehanded, is that it?"

"No."

"Well then, with my help. What's my role?"

"To get out, if you can."

"You're a warm human person after all. I've wronged you in my heart. Sure, I'll get out. I don't like this place one little bit."

"If you can get out. I think there's just a chance that the steamer may be allowed to sail for Latuan tomorrow. To keep things looking normal."

"Correction . . . today. It's now two-twenty-seven by my illuminated dial. What would happen to you if you tried to get on that ship?"

"An accident."

"Paul, in view of our close association here you don't think that same accident could happen to me?"

"Only Lee Wat saw us doing any talking. And he's out of the picture, I'm damn sure of that."

"All right, I get to Latuan. What then?"

"You make a loud noise about the need for British troops here at once."

"Coming from an American citizen that's going to be well received by British brass."

"You don't try to do anything direct. Just phone the Singapore police and ask for Inspector Kang. Be sure you get him. Tell him what I've told you. He'll do what's needed after that."

"All right, but you still don't think I'm going to be able just to sail away, do you?"

"No. There's only an outside chance."

"You don't happen to have any sleeping tablets, Paul? Like a fool I thought sudden peace and quiet would be enough. I can sleep all right directly after a Saigon bomb outrage on the press club, but there's something about the silence here that sets a clock going in my brain. Tick, tock, you'll never get home alive."

"Try counting sheep."

But it didn't work with me, either. When I finally opened the shutters onto the veranda beyond my bedroom there was light in the sky, red light and plenty of it, the shepherd's warning in the West, but dawn comes red every day out here, perhaps because the need for a warning is chronic. Red was joined by lemon-yellow and then green as I smoked, and the sea took life from its night shroud, white flecking on it, then a depth of gray-blue coming which changed to turquoise. The dawn breeze came, too, as cleansing as ever. It was the hour when insects rise above the jungle tops to dry out dampened wings and you see vast clouds of them, and hear them, too, sending out a thin, monotonous hymn to light. Not a mile away the jackals and the panthers were looking for cover, some hungry, some fed, according to their efficiency. Down below me the empty beach shouted for bathers and the sharks could come in under creaming surf to three-foot shallows, taking off the leg of a man whose body was still in sunlight.

The phone shrilled in the lobby and went on and on until I reached it.

"Paul? Is that you, Paul?" The voice broke. "They've . . ."

"Ursula?"

"They've . . . It's Charlie. He's . . . They shot him."

The noise she made was like coughing over the wires. I waited.

"Is he dead?"

"Yes." Her voice flattened out. "Yes, he's dead."

"Ursula, listen to me."

"I can't hear . . . I can't hear you very well. It's because I . . ."

I shouted.

"Have you got a car there?"

"What? What do you mean?"

[132]

"I can't get to you quickly. I haven't got a car. But get in yours and come here. Now. Come to the rest house."

"No. I'm not leaving him!"

"Ursula, for God's sake listen to me. Come here! And at once. Leave the Residency as quickly as you can. I'll go back in your car. But you get here."

"I don't see that . . . ?"

"Do what I say! Have you phoned Manson?"

"No, just you. I couldn't do that for . . . I mean I wandered around here."

"What about the servants?"

"I couldn't find them. There's no one here."

I might have made my warning to Charlie stronger. He still wouldn't have listened.

When Ursula hung up I found the liquor store and broke the lock to get brandy. Then I went out and shouted for Clem. He didn't answer and didn't join me in the kitchen while I made coffee, or on the veranda as a little green Triumph came bumping down from the highway. Charlie's wife had done what I told her and come as she was, wearing a nightgown with a raincoat over it. There was a scarf around her head and her feet were in Malay slippers, frivolously embroidered. Grief had cut sudden lines into her face, but she wasn't crying, just perspiring from the heat of the raincoat. She walked as firmly as a woman could on loose stones and in flapping slippers.

I took her arm on the steps and led her to a chair, then poured the brandy. Her big hands went around the glass and she stared at a point on the floor.

"Ursula, you knew I was there last night?"

She nodded without lifting her head.

"Did you see your husband when he was getting me something to eat?"

"Yes. He didn't see me."

"You were in the hall when I left? Listening?"

"Yes. And I spoke to Charlie when you'd gone. I didn't want him to use that radio. I thought you were trying to frighten him into it. And I was sure we could handle things here. Ourselves. I've been a fool."

"What did Charles say to you?"

"He was . . . I couldn't see his face. We didn't put on lights. He seemed angry. At you or me, I don't know. But he told me to go to bed. That he wasn't using the radio. He practically ordered me to my room."

The shock of getting an order from Charlie remained even now. She hadn't received many in her married life from that quarter.

"And did you go to bed?"

"Yes. In the dark. It's a dreadful place to walk around in without lights. I remember thinking that I didn't know why we were doing it. As though we had something to hide. And we didn't. Charles was just doing his job. I was certain that we could deal with the Sultan. Even if the phone was tapped . . ."

"How long were you in your room alone?"

"Charles never came to me at all. He may have been upstairs, I don't know. I must have slept. I didn't think I was going to, but I must have done. The shots woke me."

"Were there many of them?"

"Three or four, I think. Perhaps more. They were a long way off. I thought at first outside the building. Then I got up and went down. I used a torch. I found him . . . with the torch."

She put down the glass and covered her face with hands. I waited, then said:

"Drink the brandy."

Clem came to stand beside us.

"I was down on the beach. What's happened?"

"Take care of her, will you?" I said. "And phone the police."

Ursula's hands dropped away.

[134]

"Paul, where are you going?"

"Borrowing your car for a few minutes. I won't be away long."

"But I want to go home. Back to my house!"

"I'll take you there very soon."

I put the green Triumph fast down that road toward the ferry. Most of the way it was a neat slice out of thick jungle, with few bends, the growth on both sides making a solid-looking wall. It was the kind of jungle that used to be called militarily impenetrable until the Japanese came romping through it in Malaya and blew that little command-post theory to pieces.

The car climbed up over a ridge but there was still no view, the trees climbed with it. The drop down was sharp, with two bends, and suddenly the jungle ended in cultivated rubber, probably a Yin Tao plantation until the sell-out down in Singapore.

I didn't see the ferry until I was almost on it. The thing seemed to be waiting for custom, with the ramp down at my side of the river. It crossed on a cable with a metal arm up to this, a needed hold against the current, a flat-bottomed barge with space for two cars, driven by a big diesel engine. You couldn't see any sign of the oil concession from here, not even the derricks, for that was three miles further on, beyond more rubber and more jungle on rising ground.

I was out of the car before I noticed three men sitting in a ditch just beyond the cable mooring and they had what looked like most of the engine spread out on a rubber ground sheet.

I went over, my approach watched. My Malay was politely answered, but as though the men found me a little difficult to understand. This was routine maintenance. Every few months they took a couple of days off to strip down the engine. It was a hard-worked engine and needed the attention. There was no replacement so ferry services had to be suspended, as I would understand. It would be impossible for me to get across to visit the oil company today. Tomorrow, perhaps, if the re-assembly went to schedule.

I could feel a lack of any real urgency behind what they were doing, and it occurred to me that routine maintenance which meant a suspension of service would almost certainly be announced for the convenience of citizens. It would seem that this had been overlooked for over on the opposite bank was a Chinese vegetable lorry with the driver standing in front of it, waving his arms and presumably shouting, though we couldn't hear anything from him at all; the muddy, swift water made a lot of noise rushing to the sea.

EIGHT

BACK at the rest house I found Ursula taking refuge in that terrible practicality with which some people meet grief. Only her eyes in that applied composure suggested she realized, through his death, just how much she had loaded onto her husband in his living, making a man who had been born unequal to it carry the great weight of her ambitions. Ursula had taken a desire for power into marriage and to as remote a corner of the residual empire as could be found, nursing there a reminiscence of past family splendors, of Uncle Henry who had been the governor of an Indian province, and Uncle Will who had served out justice from dignity in the West Indies. Little Charlie had been all she had as a vehicle and she now believed she had driven him to his death. All that was left to her was to wear a kind of dignity from self-condemnation.

"I want him brought home, Paul." Her voice was calm. "Out of the Residency. Do you think you could get someone to see to that?"

"I'll see to it."

"Will you? That's kind."

I got the order of merit for kindness, solemnly awarded. I found myself wanting to help the woman, and with the knowledge that I mightn't be able to, the thing that would destroy her totally just around the corner.

She stood to be taken home herself, giving Clem a nod, as though acknowledging service received. His face had the screwed-up look of a man whose way of life has given him every reason to become tough, but who still hasn't made it.

It was the look he would have worn for a young man's living brought to an end by a Viet Cong bullet, a reaction to pain from outside yourself that some can never learn not to feel.

In the car Ursula took a cigarette. She kept staring at the instrument facia as we drove.

"I'm so glad you were here," she said. "There aren't many I could turn to in Bintan. The State Treasurer is really our only colleague left. But he's a bachelor and very withdrawn. We've never seen much of him, nor did John for that matter, socially. Though, of course, we've had him to dinner sometimes."

Protocol dinners, the State Treasurer and the Assistant Resident, both pensionable employment. I could see Ursula faintly patronizing over tinned soup to the man who had never thought it necessary to have a wife to further his interests. And their guest would leave at ten o'clock, glad to.

"I don't know your bungalow," I said.

"It's the Residency road. You just carry on up the hill."

I knew she was suddenly crying, though I didn't hear her, sitting beside me with tears running down carved cheeks, and not wanting the fact noticed. In a moment she would be ignoring the tears again, denying them.

"Charlie had the life here that suited him," I said.

It was a brick in the fiction I was starting to build for her without any way of knowing how far I could get with the construction before it was knocked flat.

"You don't have to say these things to me, Paul. The turning is the next left. It's rather a sharp angle into the drive."

There was the usual screen of jungle trees, then a garden which said at once that it wasn't just maintained by a Dyak. Ursula worked here, too, putting out roses where they wouldn't get too much sun, coaxing the English perennials that have traveled the world with conquerors and are dying away again without them, heat-blasted larkspur and the sadly

[138]

pale delphiniums, weary violets and bleached petunias. No cannas, no hibiscus, for this was England, ringed about by evergreen and the mocking hardwood giants.

There was no wall, no real defenses, but it looked somehow completely safe, as though alien violence could never penetrate into this sacred grove, the house with its sprawling verandas certain to remain immune while noise mounted down in the valley.

It was an illusion. I had seen too much that looked safe in the Far East ripped open. As a youth I had watched a society disintegrate in my own Malaya. One day the easy pattern, the clubs, the parties by swimming pools, the big cars, comfortable laughter in gardens, the next it had been the little men coming through the jungle, and the sprawling bungalows suddenly deserted in overnight panic, with silver-framed family photos sitting on grand pianos waiting for looters. My father had died then, and my brother and I barely survived.

The car stopped on gravel in front of the house. There was no sign of life in it. I thought of the Residency suddenly emptied of servants, and I knew this was in Ursula's mind, too. Then the sight of a man coming from veranda shadow was positive relief, a tall, good-looking Dyak, bowing to the woman in the car, his face solemn. Word about Charlie had reached here.

Ursula got out. The man didn't seem to notice the way she was dressed. He waited for her, erect, impeccably tidy, dignified.

"Busan . . ." she said, with gratitude.

He wasn't her servant then. I remembered, not without satisfaction, that the Dyaks are traditional enemies of the Chinese and born fighters who had chopped down the enemies of a white raja with their razor-edged parangs. Busan might very well have male relations available who would come here to help keep this place immune.

I went along the Residency corridor to the study, where the door was open. Manson was standing by the open steel shutters to the radio set. I could see that this had taken bullets, there were wires in the air, and splintered glass. Manson looked up and saw me. At once he used an aggressive anger.

"Well, Harris, what do you want? This is a police matter. We're in charge."

It was then I noticed two other men, both in uniform, a sergeant and a constable. They were looking at me, too.

"I've come from Mrs. Gissing."

"Where the hell is she? I've been trying to find her."

"Home now. She wants Charlie's body sent to her."

"It had better be sent coffined," Manson said, with flat brutality.

I looked around the door. There was a fourth man in the room, squatting down by Charlie, a young Tamil doctor with a physique so frail and so finely boned a strong wind would make anchorage a real problem. It was a good, chiseled face, almost black, and clearly the man's training at the university in Singapore hadn't quite prepared him for this kind of death. His expression held outraged protest.

Luger bullets do a lot of visible damage. Charlie had taken one in the face. That made me put out a hand for the knob and I felt the key in the lock, on the outside of the door.

Manson came across the room.

"Well, doctor? Time of death?"

"It is very difficult to establish precisely," the Tamil said in a high, thin voice.

"Ursula can do that for you."

Manson glared at me.

"What do you mean?"

"She discovered the body after hearing shots. Just before dawn. She phoned me."

"And why the hell not me?"

"You can ask her. Perhaps she wanted a friend."

"Why did Mrs. Gissing run away from here?"

"I told her to. She was nearly hysterical and quite alone. I got her to drive to the rest house."

"And after an hour or so the police are informed by some Yank tourist, is that it?"

"That's it."

His hands became fists.

"I think I'd better have a talk with you, Harris. We'll use a room somewhere."

We used the room with the canna lilies which was musty from closed windows. In a servantless house it was isolated enough and had a solid teak door to shut. Manson locked this.

"Good act," I said. "For your sergeant."

"Yes." It hurt him to admit it. "I trained the bastard."

"Always by your side?"

"That's where he's supposed to be. I think the Sultan's got Lil."

"What?"

"It's the reason I'm late getting here. I was called to the palace. Practically an official audience. I didn't get word of Charlie's killing until I got back. So my sergeant was the man on the spot."

"Manson, what do you think's happening?"

"Give me a cigarette." He almost spat out the smoke. "His Highness is greatly disturbed by the wave of crime in Bintan. Particularly kidnapping. There's only been a bit of wife snitching in the country until now and that never troubled anyone. His Highness thinks that Lil has been carried off by some gang from Sarawak. All the scoundrels come from over there; we don't breed any at home. So she is being spirited over the border to be held for ransom."

"He gave you this guff?"

"Yes, and with a great air of authority. El Badas knows. What is required now is a spot of kidnapper hunting. Up near the frontier. I'm to go at once, with half my men."

[141]

"My God!"

"You can say it. Gets me nicely out of the picture, doesn't it? It's a wonder he didn't choose the men to go with me. Leaving all his own boys, here."

"Are you going?"

"No."

"What will happen?"

"The Sultan might sack me. Or lock me up. He's an absolute monarch. None of the civil servants around here have ever tried to defy one of his direct orders, probably because John was here to keep the fat fool from issuing them."

"The ferry isn't working."

Manson showed his yellow teeth.

"Don't try to startle me, Harris. This is my beat. I was down there last night on the Lil-hunting patrol. Ferry wasn't working then either. Engine stripped down, place deserted. Except that I knew damn well there was a guard back in the rubber somewhere watching. Felt it in my bones. Boys ready to send bullets at any who tried to improvise any way of getting across. Not that you could, with that current. And there's something else that ought to interest you. There isn't a junk at anchor in the harbor. The place is swept clean."

"What about small boats?"

"They're still around. But it's my bet they're watched."

I felt it was time the policeman knew Charlie's story about the Sultan. Manson's face showed nothing.

"Are you suggesting Gissing was trying to get a message out when he was plugged?" he asked.

"If he had been why was he found behind the door? No traces of his being moved are there?"

"None at all."

"What do you know about Charlie?" I asked.

Manson answered at once.

"More than John thought I did. Quite a lot more." He

dropped the subject. "Let me congratulate you on being alive this morning."

"I had to be active to make it."

"I'm sure."

He didn't want to hear about my troubles, he had too big a plateful of his own.

"Harris, you know this as well as I do. Bintan is nicely parceled-up. I wish I'd let myself see yesterday just how tightly all the strings were being tied and shipped you out on the afternoon boat, under arrest if necessary. But with some messages from me to the outside world. I had to go on playing the Chief of Police even though I could feel their rope on my ankle, and the way they were paying it out to let me go on pretending to be active."

He struck a fist into the palm of his hand. His voice was louder than I liked.

"What the hell can I do? It would take me fifteen hours to get into Sarawak from the end of the road."

"Have you considered locking up Yin Tao?"

He stared at me.

"For years, with longing. I hate the bastard. He runs in all the opium. Our addiction rate is high. Dyaks don't begin to have the racial immunity of the Chinese. The stuff rots them. You can buy it in any eating house at Yin's rates. And with a total police force of thirty-eight men there was damn all I could do about it even before half of them were corrupted."

"So you couldn't stop junks landing anything they wanted along these coasts?"

"I've just told you, no!"

"I'm thinking of Red Chinese, Manson."

"Don't you think we've thought about it? John and I have had that nightmare for years. And if you want to know what I think is happening in little Bintan, I'll tell you. The nightmare's real. They're here. And somehow they've got el Badas in their pocket. God knows what they've promised him, but the Chinese have quite a history of handling puppets. He must have been convinced he'd be better off allied to Mao. And it's not so hard to see why, maybe, when you look around you in these parts."

"And Linau in all this?"

"She's hell's own bitch," he said, then took another of my cigarettes.

There was no trained force of European volunteers in Bintan town, not surprising in view of the eleven able-bodied men available. I suggested one of us making a break for it into the jungle, then taking a big circle up to where the river was fordable and so reaching the oil company and their radio. Manson thought this charmingly naïve. He pointed out that if the Reds were in Bintan already, and in force, they were here for one thing, to get the oil. That compound would be their main concentration, ringed with men who had worked their way through jungle, probably days ago, encircling the prize and at the moment only screened from it by the massive walls of primary forest.

"Are there no guards at the oil company?"

"Watchmen," Manson said. "That's all. Keeping an eye on the derricks. In case village kids sneak in and turn on a valve. There's wire fencing of the kind you can get through with a good cutter, but the main gates are open most of the day and night, too. A surprise attack on the place is going to find all the oil people either in their beds or wearing tropic light-weights at the company club. They wouldn't have a chance to resist and I hope they don't get one. Because it would mean a massacre and nothing else. There are plenty of women and kids in those flower-decked, air-conditioned bungalows."

Manson saw a timed attack hitting the oil company and Bintan town at the same moment. He was certain it was set for tonight.

"Harris, I suggest you go back to the rest house and put in

some serious thinking about how you can survive. The American and you might just manage. I don't rate your chances high, but you're unarmed, nonbelligerents."

I didn't tell him about John's guns.

"And you?"

"Death or glory boy, that's me. There are three places where I just might get a boat that would take me to the oil company radio."

"In daylight?"

"That's my little hazard. I have no relations who would appreciate a last message from me, so I don't have to trouble you on that score."

"Wouldn't it be better if we stuck together?"

"Not for you, it wouldn't. Especially after I've stepped out of office as Chief of Police. And here endeth my interrogation of a possible suspect in a Gissing murder. Best of British luck in the hours to come."

He showed his teeth again before going over to the door and opening it. The passage into the hall seemed empty enough, but Manson still raised his voice for a possible audience.

"Mr. Harris, you'll go back to the rest house and wait there. I'll want you later for further questioning."

As his shoes clicked away I wondered how effective that had sounded. Not very. When I got to the main entrance area myself the sergeant was standing there, apparently on duty. He wasn't the type I'd have chosen for advanced training myself. I didn't like his pockmarked face.

I stepped out into sunlight, and as I did it there was a hooting. The Residency gardens had a fine view of the harbor and right in the middle of this was the steamer from Latuan, a four-hundred-ton veteran of other seas and better days, with a list, and from the funnel smoke still a coal burner. She was coming to us from the world, bringing mail and provisions and probably a selection of seasick locals back from visits to cosmopolitan Latuan where planes landed and took off. They couldn't land in Bintan until the oil company jet strip was finished in about six months, or more quickly under Chinese overseers of labor who wouldn't hesitate to tie a lazy Dyak up to a palm tree and flog him. The boat was early.

At the driver's door of the green Triumph a shuffling sound made me turn. They were bringing what was left of Charlie out on a blanket-covered stretcher, with the Tamil doctor walking behind, still looking like a man who doesn't believe that people ought to die in this way. They put the stretcher in at the back of an ambulance which suggested an old army reject, with a rear door that couldn't be shut properly. The contraption bumped away down the drive on soft tires, a final comment on a little man's ambitions.

Clem was in the rest house kitchen eating bread, butter and sardines.

"Brunch," he said. "And in half an hour I've got the community taxi coming for me. Any sign of my ship?"

"Yes, it's in."

"And does it go out again?"

"The odds are five hundred to one against, but you'd better make the gesture of going down there."

"And when I come back?"

I smiled at him.

"It'll be to face a simple choice. I've got a couple of rifles upstairs to let us make a last stand like men. Or we can wave our passports and demand the protection of the local representative of Thomas Cook and Sons. The choice is yours."

"I choose the passport waving," Clem said.

"I thought you would. But there's quite a chance that no one in the Red expeditionary force will have heard of Thomas Cook."

He stared at me.

"Somehow I took you for the kind of character who always

kept one jump ahead of the opposition with a plan."

"That's me. And I've got a really neat idea. You're not a long-distance swimmer by any chance?"

"I can do a nifty sidestroke that conserves energy. Why?"

"I'm looking for someone who'll swim about a mile out to sea to counter the currents at the river mouth and then swim in again to call on the oil company."

"What about the shark hazard?"

"It's right there. That's why I'm not detailing you off for this assignment. Just calling for volunteers."

Clem swallowed another sardine.

"I don't understand why you people ever lost your Empire with your remarkable gift for getting others to do your dirty work. It must have been sheer carelessness."

I cut myself a piece of bread and buttered it. Then I put Clem in the full picture. He listened carefully.

"I resent the idea of dying tonight," he said.

"So do I."

"Isn't there a fort we could man, Paul? I thought you imperialists always laid on a fort in which you carried on with the muzzle loading even when the flag was shot away?"

"There is no fort in Bintan."

"There must be something better than this place. You only make a last stand out on the veranda in a cowboy movie. And any medium-caliber bullet is going to go straight through these walls. You don't think they'll have landed any artillery? Or a few tanks?"

"Big mortars, certainly."

"I'm sorry, but I just don't like this cause. It doesn't seem to me worthy."

"There's an argument for it. These are Chinese Reds."

"Against these odds there is no argument. How many do you think have landed?"

"One battalion. Two. It could have been going on quietly for months. All they had to do was land and go into the jungle. And sit there, waiting. Polishing their bullets. To say nothing of bayonets."

Clem opened a can of beer and it spurted.

"You haven't left me any sardines," I said.

"There's another tin. I don't know how you can eat at a time like this."

He sat on a stool smoking and looking out of the kitchen at the quarters Lee Wat had evacuated. There was a certain dereliction in this view, an area until only recently devoted to packed human activity now empty, its silence a prophecy.

"How was Mrs. Gissing when you left her?"

"Calm," I said.

"I felt sorry for that old horse. What happens to the women and children around here when the shooting starts?"

"I hope they stay in their houses. With their men."

"I see. Just you and me as an Anglo-American duet to take on the whole Chinese assault?"

"We've got a policeman helping us."

"His sounds like a suicide detail to me."

"Manson would agree with you."

"There's a laugh in this somewhere if I can find it."

But neither of us could find it. We hadn't said a word in ten minutes when a car horn hooted. Clem stood.

"Well, General, if that boat sails with me on it I'll stay in Latuan long enough to write a story of your handling of this campaign that will go right round the world. And earn me three thousand dollars, plus expenses."

"Thanks."

Clem smiled.

"I never wanted au revoir to mean goodbye more than I do now."

We went out on the veranda. His bags and typewriter were already there. The driver came up the steps to take the luggage and I noticed that all the time he was near the man never gave us one look. I was certain Clem would be back but I began to get that left-behind feeling even while the car was still churning up dust in the court.

I sat down and put my feet up on the railing like a last survivor in a ghost town who is making free use of the crumbling saloon and hotel. I had plenty of time to take a look at the general picture and details of this had suddenly become painfully clear. I agreed with Manson that the attack would come at night. There were a number of reasons for this, the main one being that it is much easier to capture a town asleep than one awake. There is a fair chance that if noise is kept down some of the citizens at least will go on sleeping, waking to a *fait accompli*, a new order established. And a shock before breakfast tends to become slightly absorbed by the first food of the day. Business as usual then becomes the natural reaction, or an attempt at business as usual, and there is something emotionally sedative about going to the office in the ordinary way, or opening up your eating house. The sun is bright and it is patent that life goes on, taking you with it. You do notice the Chinese soldiers posted in front of municipal buildings and at street corners, but the first radio news has announced that the men in tin hats are friends of the new Bintanese nation. Rich businessman Yin Tao has let it be known that the *towkays* are all in favor of the new democracy. The men in tin hats are certainly carrying guns, and these worn with blunt fingers near triggers, but this is only to preserve order during the transitional period while independence is being firmly established. You may have left your wife weeping in the kitchen, but women always look on the worst side and it's a man's duty to ignore extremes of emotionalism. So three cheers for the great father el Badas who will speak to all again later on in the morning.

So easy, so damned easy, in a little country where communications to the frontiers have been carefully kept primitive over the years and the seacoast has been dealt with. I tried to tell myself that el Badas would never get away with his new and sudden alliance to six hundred million Chinese, that the U.S. fleet was cruising around out there almost within calling-distance and that we had a lot of planes in Singapore. The basic military situation could be said to be in the West's favor but, sadly, there were other factors. The most important of these was that declaration of independence. It was going to get us an awfully bad press with the uncommitted nations if we started another war in a little Far Eastern country by landing troops to depose the regime in power, this against the democratically expressed will of the Bintanese people, the few who could read and the majority who couldn't. The extreme left in Britain would immediately begin to make howling noises of their own. The Colonial Secretary would have a sleepless night and so would the Minister of War. The P.M. would rise in the House to remind us of our solemn treaty obligations to an accompaniment of howls from bright, forward-looking young men in the back benches. A minority in Britain, but a noisy one, would tell the world that if Bintan wanted to go Red that was their business.

There was also the matter of oil. Mention that slime and half the world goes into automatic shouts about capitalist exploitation. And unfortunately oil would be the basic issue, for us and for the Chinese.

The situation could, of course, be totally changed if British troops landed before or even just immediately after the el Badas appeal to the world, when things would be still highly confused, to put it mildly. Our forces would then be operating in a protectorate where they had a legal right to be under international law and where Chinese troops had no right to be at all, since they could scarcely claim that they had responded quite so quickly to a call for help from a Far Eastern brother. In these circumstances they ran the risk of being branded invaders even by the Afro-Asian bloc, some of whom, thank God, are getting a bit jumpy about Chinese intentions in the world at large.

After all, the protected can't really expect to get away with an overnight call for a new protector. If our troops arrived in time the British permanent representative at the U.N. could say in the Assembly that what was happening was only a local police action to restore order in a territory suddenly threatened by Red guerrilla action. And a very nice speech he could make of it, too, backed by the knowledge that when both sides have troops in a piece of disputed territory there is a fair chance of a straight fight to decide the issue before international interference grinds into action. Also, in this particular case, Chinese troops might be on the spot, but they couldn't expect to be supplied, either from the air or from the sea.

As a Malaysian I had my own angle on all this. The oil royalties of a Federated Bintan would help our balance of trade a good deal, which put me in the very strong moral position of being able to serve two loyalties at the same time, the old one and the new. I had no ethical problem to disturb me at all, just the very simple one of what the hell could I do?

The idea which came then was the one I had put to Manson only to have it dismissed as impractical. It still seemed to me that the river, which needed a big power plant to get you across near its mouth, might be fordable somewhere not too far up in the jungle. And one man, after a lot of walking and much caution, could just possibly slip through the entrenched Chinese and end up strolling into the oil compound looking as though he had come to play tennis.

I took my feet off the veranda railing and just as I did the road beyond was much livened-up by the first piece of traffic to move along it since my return to the rest house. This was an open-sided truck laden with dry-goods merchandise making back for Bintan after what was clearly an attempt to cross the ferry for trade with the rich oil company wives. An air of prosperity about the mobile shop suggested that business over there was usually good. Freshly painted on the cab door was "Ayab Chikamongerjee, Household Essentials and Novelties." The driver must have spotted me for he braked and hopped down, a neat little Tamil of the kind who has long survived in all parts of the Far East by learning to put up the shutters of his shop at the first signs of political unrest but taking them down again niftily the moment there is the slightest chance of business as usual.

I rather felt that this was Mr. Chikamongerjee himself, and he was coming too fast for any escape.

"Tuan, please! What is happening now, then?"

He reached the steps and ran up them, a fervent small capitalist in white whose whole life had been devoted to the profit motive, sometimes under difficult circumstances. He was sweating as he stood before me.

"You are knowing, Tuan?"

"What?"

"This morning I am calling to the oil company. On the telephone, you see. But I am not getting. No, never. They say I am not to get. So I go in my lorry to ferry, you see. And there I am not going also. You understand?"

I understood only too well.

"You are knowing what is to happen, Tuan?"

"I'm only a visitor to Bintan."

He couldn't accept the tourist status for a European, perhaps because he had seen so few of them.

"Why is this no ferry? Why is this not told to us?"

I said I didn't know, hating the lie. Once, under the umbrella of Pax Britannica, there were many thousands of Chikamongerjees, the majority of them now disillusioned and more than that, the casualties of change, little men, hard-working, fairly honest, in a way the servants of a stable order if sometimes usurers in it. I could see terror in the eyes peering at me.

Then he turned away and darted into the rest house, as though sensing its emptiness. I heard him blundering around in there and once his voice. He came back, shaking. The more extrovert form of courage was no part of his equipment and he made no pretense.

"Tuan, you are telling me? Please, you are telling me! Lee Wat not here. No one here. You tell me. Tuan, I have little babies, so."

He staged them with his hand, from the veranda floor upward, bending down for the youngest, rising slowly as his hand came up, his eyes always on my face.

"Trouble coming, Tuan? Trouble?"

"Mr. Chikamongerjee, go back to your shop. You'll be fine."

My assurance was like an official handout. He'd experienced these before. For all I knew the man could be a refugee from other troubles, who had just managed to make the last ship out and could never forget that feeling. There would be no last ship from Bintan.

He was angry at me before he went away. It only just showed, a flickering in his eyes, the kind of look you get in the East these days which sets up a faint crawling at the back of your neck. You know perfectly well then what kind of mercy you could expect if the supplicant ever became commissar. Not much. So many don't love us in the area that it can get to be quite a weight on your living if you allow yourself much thinking about it.

I watched him drive off, the bright van shining with the optimism of achieved success until it was swallowed by jungle green. Then I went out to the kitchen and started to make myself food which I was going to need as a cross-country hiker. This meant opening tins. The place was well stocked and if I'd been up to it I could have turned out a real gourmet menu. I opened the fridge to find that stocked, too, mostly with bowls of what looked like long-preserved curries all congealed in yellow fat. I brought baked beans to the boil for spreading on stale bread toast and was stirring the pan when I was conscious of someone just beyond the open doorway to the passage for the lobby, someone too short to be Clem, someone just standing there, but not empty-handed.

He got boiling beans in his face as the gun went off. The bullet made a lot of noise up on a shelf of pots, but not as much noise as the man was making. He swayed back into the dim passage, waving an automatic rifle about but not yet able to use it. I went for his legs and he started to come down, but was quicker than I'd expected with the rifle as a club. It didn't get my head and your back can take a lot. I punched him twice and no Queensberry rules. He had stopped screaming to get his breath and I heard his breathing, close to mine.

A little man like a monkey, but much tougher than Lee Wat, all muscles massaged by a lot of exercise, tight-scrapping steel. He was accustomed to close combat, too, and had let the rifle go to use what nature had given him, with training.

I don't quite know what happened to me. Maybe the Chinese army has evolved a new secret judo. The little man was limp for seconds, then arched tight, his body like an upthrusting old wooden bridge and feeling as solidly based. This broke under hammering, but not as completely as I expected. There was a flip and I was over. He was top boy, with a splayed, thrashing efficiency of arms and legs which was unpleasant to experience. I couldn't stop him getting hold of my head and using it against the skirting board like a football. After about the fifth crack I could feel resistance going, a tap turned off, and consciousness with it.

He didn't go on trying to kill me that way, perhaps earlier victims had recovered from concussion. There was, instead, a serene moment of peace, when the brief violence seemed dreamily remote. I opened my eyes.

It was still dim in the passage but the light from the kitchen showed the man, a little man who liked his work. He was wearing jungle-green daubed with camouflage marks and there were beans still on his face and down the front of his tunic. He was grinning, and had very good teeth to do it with. In his hands was the automatic rifle, pointing down, a finger already stroking the trigger.

The only decision left to me was to open or shut my eyes, I had that choice. I kept them open and was looking straight into the little round hole of death when there was a crack beyond, quite sharp, decisive, but not too loud. The round hole jerked up and the killer's body came down on mine. I knew somehow that it was a dead body before I stopped thinking.

NINE

WHEN I have to stay in a room for any length of time I do things to it, pushing the furniture about, automatically rejecting other people's arrangements for me. I'm defeated only by contemporary interior decorators whose rooms remain immune to any pushing around, boxes for existing in which defy any attempt to make them personal. Give any of these boys one glass wall and three other plain ones, preferably with a balcony beyond twenty stories up which is handy to jump off when you can't stand any more, and they can create anywhere in the world an esthetic negative which is one of the unique achievements of twentieth-century man. I have to live in these rooms all the time because any other kind are rapidly disappearing, and in them I have experienced all my worst moments, when my life was dust and continued living pointless. You wake in an air-conditioned cell mated by inadequate partitioning to half a hundred similar cells in which lie half a hundred other near-corpses trying to move back far enough from total dissolution to ring for room service. You stay still for quite some time knowing that you are totally and forever alone even though a wife in curlers is occupying the next sleeping unit. And the most horrible thing of all is that the magazines, the architects, and characters who know better than you, are hard at work trying to turn homes into these units, too, scientifically insulating them against the smell of frying bacon and other horrors of old-fashioned domesticity.

Is it any wonder that so many of us are developing a kind

of Freudian thing against waking up at all? We are naturally reluctant to come back from pill-induced sleep to reach for the daily vitamin intake essential for the waiting contest with other top people. I find myself, away from the home which is still security to my subconscious, opening one eye cautiously to test environment before I risk using the other one.

I did that. The second eye popped open.

It was quite a room I saw, lush with triumphant individuality, a room in which the decor was a shout of tropic baroque flamboyance and where scientific planning had never even got a nose around the door. The bed in which I lay was a barque in which to sail on long voyages of exploration into the pleasures of the night, huge, clearly on a dais, floating slightly above the exotic anchorage which held it. Drawn-back mosquito curtains made an elaborate pattern of barge draperies, and beyond these I saw carved screens, long doors delicately wrought in wood filigree and mirrors with frames embossed by excited animals. There were a great many fabrics worked in gold and silver thread, including the coverlet over me which was an embroidered dragon writhing in acute indigestion.

It was some time before I noticed the girl, a very ordinary Dyak girl, with black hair drawn severely back and her sarong a domestic brown. Her best feature was brown eyes, surprisingly large, watching me with timid interest. When I moved slightly, testing pieces of myself, and finding my body naked under that cover, she was up like a fawn in the wood and gone before my eyes could move to follow the flight.

It hurt to turn my head. Exploring hands found a picturesque turban of bandages. I half shut my eyes again and lay there expecting a visitor, certain who it would be and, as so often happens in this life, quite wrong. It was Lil I saw by the side of my bed, and then at the foot of it, the girl tentative and not a little frightened, if no fawn.

"Hello," I said, and she jumped.

[157]

"Oh!"

"It's all right. I'm fine, just taking it easy."

I was conscious of a lot of light in the room, all of it artificial.

"What time is it?"

"Sunset."

"Hell!" I said, and sat up.

The experiment was not a success. Nausea was something too violent to be controlled and I had to go limp again, back on pillows.

"Put out some of those lights, Lil."

"Yes. You mustn't move."

"You're the doctor?"

"No. Linau said . . ."

She stopped, waiting for my surprise. It didn't come.

"You know where you are?" Lil asked.

"I can guess."

"Did you guess I was here?"

"Yes."

"How?"

"I snooped in your room. Found a photo album. With the lady's picture out. That gave me all sorts of ideas."

I could look at her now, watching as she moved around dimming lights. The one near the chair she used was left on, as though Lil was exposing herself for me to see. The ash can make-up was gone. It was as if she was in that transitional phase still where she could step from the child into the aggressive armor of adolescence and back again at will. She was back again now and I liked it much better, a reduction—if temporary—in the area of my problem.

"Linau saved your life," Lil said. "She shot that man."

"I must remember to thank her. Where is she now?"

"I don't know." But I had the feeling she did. "Uncle Paul, I had to run away from the Residency. Do you understand? I just had to. It was Charlie Gissing. The way he went on, being so damn nice to me."

There was just a flick of Boots Kinsley's girl in the way she said that.

"Nice about what?"

"About not blaming me for Daddy. Ursula wasn't so bad, but Charlie . . ."

"You know he's dead?"

"Yes."

There was no politeness of regret.

"I thought you'd jaw at me, too."

"Have I ever?"

"I suppose not. But how was I to know? You loved Daddy. And . . . I felt absolutely alone, do you understand that?"

"Yes."

The unbearable when you're young, the thing to be defeated at all cost.

"It was hell in their house and it was hell going back to the Residency. I couldn't let you in when you knocked. I couldn't!"

"You thought I was an escort jailer?"

She sniffled.

"You wouldn't understand about Boots. How could you? I didn't want to leave Bintan. Because . . ."

"You'd been in touch with your boy friend and he was coming to collect you?"

"How did you know that?"

"Kinsley would obviously write. I didn't think Ursula was steaming open your letters. Did you get in touch by phone to Singapore?"

"Yes. Boots wasn't in the hotel. I had to get him to ring me back."

"Why wasn't that call to the Residency picked up by anyone?"

"Because I used the private line to Daddy's study. And fixed a time when I knew Charlie wouldn't be in there. Though he used it enough. He took over and sat in Daddy's chair."

"You were out and about in the house quite a bit."

She stared at the floor.

"All right, I was."

"Lil, do you know anything about your father's death?"

"No. I didn't even hear the gun. I must have been playing a record. That's a laugh, isn't it?"

She put her hands over her face, a young girl's hands, no lacquer on the nails, which looked chewed.

"I thought Linau could tell me something. And she did. She told me that daddy didn't kill himself. Do you believe that?"

"Yes."

The hands came away. She stared at me.

"Then why was Charlie . . . ?"

"Lil, Charlie's dead. There is no use asking why he did anything. Can you get me a drink?"

"Oh, yes. Linau said you might want whisky. It's here."

"Make it half water."

She brought me the glass. I had a swallow and at once knew I was going to be sick. Linau must have thought of that, too, for when I told Lil a basin appeared in seconds right under my chin. A moment or two later I said:

"I'm sorry."

Oddly it seemed to make me human to the girl. She took away the basin as calmly as a post-surgical nurse to a bathroom behind one of the screens from which I heard sounds. She brought the basin back again and bravely offered me more whisky. The second shot was sedative.

"Lil, I've got a friend at the rest house, an American . . ."

"He's here. In the sitting room. He was terribly hungry."

Quite a house party, with Linau playing mum somewhere

in the background. Only I couldn't quite see it that way.

"Has Linau told you anything about what's happening in Bintan?"

"She said there might be trouble for a day or two and it was best we were here."

"And after that we just go home?"

"I suppose so."

"Did Shah Valli say anything to you about your father's death?"

She shook her head.

"No, not really. But I had the feeling after that he'd wanted to. That he was sort of trying. But I guess I wasn't . . . oh, I was a mess. I just kept howling."

The little girl howling for daddy. I wished John could have known.

"Why choose Linau to come to?"

She looked at me again, standing quite still to do it, with the conscious dramatic effect of a bad actress in her big scene.

"Linau and Daddy were lovers."

That was supposed to explode all over me. It had, as a matter of fact, been in my mind for some time as a reasonable possibility. John and the Princess might be antagonists on occasion, but there is a considerable attraction in that state of things.

"Aren't you surprised?"

"Of course. When did you find out?"

"The night before I went to England . . . the last time."

The little girl Lil then, with no hint of a Boots Kinsley any-where, little girl about to be shipped off from the Residency for the last phases of school, away from home, away from daddy, back to loving aunts who were nonetheless childless themselves and thought of growing up as something connected with holiday treats and meeting other attractive young people of the same age group and from the right social background. It hadn't ever happened to me, but I had seen it often enough, the child sophisticates in travel, getting in airplanes with non-chalance to fly to the other side of the world where they would be alone with teachers and the ministering, just slightly burdened near-relations.

John had probably been right in his guilt feelings over these separations, the inevitable, because there was nothing you could do but accept them. It wasn't so easy to accept the fact that the young grow in spurts and one of the spurts could happen to yours in that period when you were half the globe away.

The last night in Bintan of that child Lil, the child who couldn't sleep, who in the morning would wear her fears disguised but in a tropic dark felt them beating at her, monstrous and potent, and had got out of bed to go padding along a terrazzo-tiled passage only to see the door of John's room open and Linau come out.

It was three in the morning. Lil had learned enough extra to her curriculum at school to know what that meant, and had hidden to see an idol fall, the great figure of shining, celibate daddy, more than the ruler of his house, but of a people, too, betrayed now as parents often are by ordinary humanity. She had gone back to her room and torn out that photo, her only gesture, nothing said, and the next day had climbed into the first plane at Latuan, seeming confident about where she had to go, but having no place to go at all. Her crying now echoed that desolation.

Suddenly she blew her nose.

"I couldn't understand," she said. "I just couldn't."

"And now?"

She looked straight at me.

"Of course I do! Since Boots."

God in heaven! The great love that made all other great loves comprehensible.

"Why didn't you show him this in America?"

"Because . . . he was acting like a father-figure!"

"And you knew he wasn't?"

"Yes, I did. I couldn't see it that he was just angry. I couldn't talk to him. Boots tried to, he did! Daddy just hit him. I was sick then. I didn't think he wanted to talk to me. He never showed that he did. We just sat on that plane, all the way across the Pacific. I nearly shouted at him that I knew all about Linau."

"Why didn't you? It might have done a lot of good."

She nodded.

"I know. I just didn't, that's all. I just didn't."

"Did you take up with Boots to show your father?"

"No, no!"

"How did you meet the boy?"

"At a party."

So easy these days, when guitar players go everywhere.

"Didn't you think you were a bit young to become his mistress?"

"I didn't think about it. It happened. And don't go all uncle on me. I don't want to be yapped at."

"I don't yap about things that have happened."

"Good. Then we can understand each other."

It was the understanding that was going to be the problem, she was so full of it. The one idol had gone, another had been constructed only recently, also with feet of clay, John and Linau, two shining figures instead of one, a splendid romanticism which bore not the slightest relation to any possible facts. Linau certainly hadn't lost her all in John's death, and a special relation made dramatic by a gulf of race, position and background was something I couldn't begin to imagine between two dedicated egotists who had made sex together and probably enjoyed it, full stop. Linau had seen how totally unbearable the truth would be and withheld it. For Lil the liaison had to be a secret marriage of true hearts and true minds set against a background of the exotic which made it somehow splendidly tragic. All the erotic sentimentality of recent history was on her side, propping up the new double idol that was half living, half dead.

"You had quite a talk with Linau?"

"Yes!" That was triumphant. "I'm going to marry Boots. I told her."

Legal bliss, a bit belated, but happy forever after and nothing to worry about if you started off with real passion. Much of the world would be rooting for Lil, too, and she looked as though she knew this. For my part I couldn't see a good marriage starting off with only a guitar and a synchronized bounce on a mattress as its basic ingredients.

The tart is the contemporary heroine, and this really isn't in the slightest the fault of Lil's generation, just the orgasmic climax—or let's hope it's the climax, with a nice restful semi-puritanical reaction about due—to a process which has been going on since my father's time in the twenties, gathering momentum all along the way to us, swelled periodically by yet another new "freedom" made socially acceptable. The surprising thing isn't the number of teen-agers who sex and dope, but rather that with the conditioning they've had from our world, and the world before us, that there are so many who don't. It's a shade difficult for the contemporary parent, or uncle, to go all holy without having the bluff called, as Lil had called John's even though he never knew. I was, in these moments, made sharply conscious of just how hard it is to strike attitudes of virtue when one's own patterns, and for all to see, have been pretty dubious, and the immediate effect on me of Lil's weirdly distorted phallic romanticism was one of acute uneasiness.

I wondered if even Linau had felt this, and had seen as I was doing now that Lil was the kind of girl who would have to be badly bruised before there was any crack in her fantasy armor that would allow sense to penetrate. It was clearly a case of waiting until this happened before really trying to help

[164]

at all, a negative position which puts a strain on being a guardian, and a certain shame, too. You neglect your obvious immediate duty in order to achieve it ultimately, a shaky compromise.

My head was aching. I had some more whisky to settle that and then suggested I could do with some clothes.

"Everything you had on was spattered with blood," Lil said, not without a certain zest.

"There's bound to be something to wear in this house."

"You mean something of daddy's? He never came here at all. They always used the Residency, it was safer."

That, too, rather winded me. I had resort to a first cigarette since return to consciousness.

Eventually we found a brocade curtain that would do as a sarong and, like the Edwardian I probably am at heart and may be in practice, I ordered Lil out of the room while I got shakily from the bed and swathed the thing around me. Mild concussion, if it was that, didn't like what I was doing at all, but I kept on with it, getting into a passage and from that to Linau's huge sitting room.

This was quieter than the one I had just left, but not exactly restrained, and from plaster deities molded into the decor I realized that I was in one of those Chinese rococo palaces which rich *towkays* have plopped down all over the tropic Far East, many of them abandoned these days to changed tastes. Linau's remodeling for her use had left intact all the better flights of fancy, just muting them a little, though a sculptured group over a doorway of one Chinese gentleman and two Chinese ladies having a ball had been gently lit-up.

Clem didn't see me at first and Lil wasn't in there.

"Hi," I said, not loud.

He rose and stared.

"Jehosophat! Salaams and all that. You really get into the mood of your environment."

[165]

"It's the secret of adapting yourself. Help me to a chair, Clem, I'm feeble. And fetch the whisky from back in there, will you? Are you glad now you didn't sail?"

"No. This is a gilded prison."

"How come?"

"Guards, boy, guards. We're confined to the seraglio. For future use, maybe."

"No one's going to use me for a long, long time. Where are the guards?"

"Outside that door. And one down the passage. They have those curved choppers. Look like butchers."

When he came back with the whisky I said:

"Lil seems very much at home."

"Sure, she's become one of the girls."

"Were you invited or were you brought?"

"I was brought. The taxi got me back to the rest house just about in time to see smoke rising from guns. This made me a witness who had to be forcibly entertained. Madame's chauffeur used a lethal weapon as a persuader and one look told me that the lady was far too beautiful to be good. I was persuaded to help carry you to the car. You weigh a lot. Since then I've been given food and a record player, but I'm not happy. Who wants to listen to classic jazz at a time like this?"

"You don't know whether anything's been happening in the town?"

"No. All I can tell you is there's a forty-foot drop from this harem to the garden below. You can try it if you want to. I won't. I've got weak ankles."

There was a fancy box of Linau's cheroots on the table beside me and I tried one as an experiment, which went better than I expected.

"You've put on an awfully cute act for me, Clem. But I'm afraid it's going to stop."

He had been looking out at the cheerful innocence of the town lights. He didn't turn.

[166]

"What's all this?"

"Well, for one thing I've been knocked out a few times, but I think the longest I've ever taken to come round was about twenty minutes. Also, I came to with a different kind of taste in my mouth. I don't know what drug was used to keep me inactive from two in the afternoon until sunset; all I know is that Linau and you gave me something."

He came around then, quite slowly, and the look on his face was kindly.

"Did I hear you say Linau and me?"

"That's right. Shall we get it over quickly? I think that a very short time ago indeed you were called into shore-based U.S. Naval Intelligence Saigon on about ten minutes' notice to travel. I say Naval Intelligence because that's a bright guess. This kind of action seems more in their area than Army. Anyway, you were told that a red signal had just come in, and were flown to a U.S. carrier in the South China Sea, and there briefed. The red signal was from the little island of Latuan, sent in by a Princess en route home who had just been sitting beside me in a plane."

The kindly look had changed to one of concern.

"Boy, you're delirious."

"No, my brain's just had a good shake-up. And a lot of things have fallen into place as a result."

"Just a minute, friend. I'm an American citizen, okay? And this is British territory."

"There are times when the Anglo-American alliance is quite real. Even in intelligence. And you could get here a lot quicker from Saigon than anyone could from Singapore. Also, another Briton arriving here at the moment would be looked at very hard. Much harder than an American tourist with a color camera."

"I can see we're going to need professional assistance with your case. I told Linau she ought to get a doctor. But I'm just a prisoner around here."

"You're a character who was landed on Latuan, very quietly I should think, for there wouldn't be time to push you in by one of the normal air routes. Probably a beach somewhere, a neat landing of Clement P. Winburgh, with spectacles, typewriter and a beautiful cover story about being a journalist getting away from it all."

"I am a journalist."

"But not getting away from it all. Not just at this strategic moment when the Chinese are about to make a take-over bid for little Bintan. I admit your cover is lovely, but then everyone in the business has to have really test-proof cover these days. I'll bet you one thing, Clem, your output of articles back to States has been on the thin side in the last year or two."

There was a change in his face then, the concern replaced by a blankness. He stared at me.

"Have you been checking up on my literary output?"

"No, I've been out of touch with my command post."

Clem walked over to the table and helped himself to a cheroot. He picked up the solid-silver Ronson lighter and flicked, sucking at the rolled leaf as though it was a cigarette.

"So you've got a command post?" he suggested.

"Something you've never quite been able to confirm? In spite of intensive research into the matter by your own command post? It wouldn't surprise me if one of three very tidy searches of my new Kuala Lumpur office and my home in the city had been organized by an American staff in Saigon. Actually, your department, N.I.S.A. But they drew a blank, didn't they? Because you see I'm a businessman and my files are as sweetly innocent as any Rotarian's. Which I'd think is a helluva lot more that can be said for yours. I think you're a big noise, Clem."

"This command post of yours . . . ?"

"Just kidding. Though I've had some experience in areas akin to yours. Would you like a bit of constructive criticism?"

"Why, sure."

"Using a Luger to shoot Charlie was a mistake. Not a big mistake, but one nonetheless."

Down in the town a Chinese must have been celebrating his birthday or a lottery win. A single firecracker went up to burst in a portion of black sky I could see from where I sat, a pretty umbrella of colored sparks, red, yellow, green. Clem didn't look at it.

"So you're making me a killer now?"

"And no amateur."

"I like your compliments. Why don't you like Lugers?"

"They're big and messy. Also, it's an outside weapon in these parts, not Commie, not Stateside. Your bright boys fell over backwards being subtle when they equipped you. A routine issue would have been better. Because the black markets out here are teeming with U.S. and Commie issues. About the one thing you can't buy easily is a Luger. To me it identified the user as being awfully neutral in the job he was doing. Though of course I may be wronging you and you didn't bring a gun in at all. You certainly haven't got a two-way radio, I searched your room pretty carefully for that. I suppose Linau could have loaned you the weapon needed?"

"I'm sorry about this," Clem said. "It's going to be a psychiatric ward. Delusions of grandeur. British businessman in Malaysia thinks American intelligence is after him."

"Not after me, just checking up, where others had tried and failed before. Almost a matter of professional pride."

"Paul, move over to the sofa and have a good rest."

"I've had it. Enforced. And I'm beginning to feel my old self, except for the costume. Grateful, too. After all, Linau and you looked after me. She's a trained shot all right. It's not so easy to kill a man first go with a handbag gun."

Clem's hand came up.

"Wait a minute now, wait. Let's stick to Charlie. You say I shot him. Why?"

"Because he caught you trying to use the Residency radio.

[169]

Charlie was under sentence already, deferred sentence as a Red operator. There won't be any trouble in London about you doing the job. I think you had your instructions. There won't even be a scrambled telephone call from Washington."

"My God, this is wonderful!"

"It's the truth and you know it. Charlie had the study locked on the hall side. He came in, found you at the set, and shot at the set. You shot at *him*."

"You're not even allowing me self-defense?"

"No. It was an execution."

The Chinese party sent up another firecracker. This time it was a zip rocket that had to be destroyed before it got into orbit and went bang. You could almost, but not quite, hear the voices below acclaiming that, faint sound like a murmur of palms, though there was no wind.

"I came here equipped with the combination of those steel doors?"

"I never said anything about a combination lock on those doors. Are you getting rattled, Clem? Actually Linau told you how to open up."

He threw his cheroot away. It went across the small roofed balcony and down into the garden.

"You're making me feel the convalescent now," he said. "I've got a headache. Me in cahoots with a princess, and a beautiful one at that? My mother wouldn't have liked the situation at all."

"None of our mothers would have liked our situations. They lived in a much simpler world. Clem, I haven't had a lot to go on, just little pieces sticking out that wouldn't be pushed back. Things like Charlie telling me half truths, about el Badas ready to start something. I knew very well that this had to be half true because Charlie wasn't the sort capable of truly creative invention. Not on short notice and without help. He did pretty well for Charlie, and thought so himself. But he stopped purring when I told him about that mike in the

[170]

phone. I'd swear he hadn't known about that. He wasn't just shocked that I'd found out, he was winded himself. It meant one of two things for Charlie, the Reds had put that mike in recently to check up on him or they had put the thing there long ago to check on John, without telling their man in the office. Either way it was pretty plain that he didn't have the trust of his new masters. And the poor little fool had believed until right then that he was really important to them. In most ways he was an innocent."

Clem just went on looking at me, his control perfect. I tested it slightly.

"It must have been quite a shock to you, hurrying back from your night's work at the Residency to find yourself being asked to look after the wife of the man you'd just killed."

Nothing moved in his face at all.

"Clem, I'd say I'd brought you to the position where you have to play executioner again. Or put me in the picture."

It was a moment before he spoke.

"I'm not authorized to shoot you, Paul."

TEN

I'VE worn a sarong often enough, mostly to sleep in, but some-times for a more active role on one of my junks, and I've never felt a fool with my chest bare and my legs draped. But with my back to Clem, out on that little balcony beyond Linau's sit-ting room, I felt a fool all right, dressed for the part, even after I'd taken off that turban bandage and chucked the thing down into the darkness of a walled garden. I felt a fool from an innocence that was period and dated, but used nonetheless with determination as a screen against the real furies of my world. I'd used it while I played at participation, going on those solo treks that involved some danger but now, on this black night, seemed no more than an exhibitionist escapism.

Clem had called my bluff and I hated him for it.

It was the flaring hatred of a child rebelling against punish-ment suddenly meted out by an adult whose authority isn't acceptable. I stood staring down at a town gone dead in sleep, its lights out now, seeing myself as John must have seen me, the playboy, the continuing adolescent suspended in his own activities, surrounded by the toys that pleased him, fast cars, a smooth surface to living, and just under this, but not very far under, the synthetic adventure pattern, my junks with armor plating on the bows, my sudden journeys about which I never talked, maintaining the held mystery of my absences. I could see, too, the success I'd had as an accident of circumstance, largely an inheritance from my father and after him my brother, money which I managed to swell because I had an administrative knack and a flair for making the fairly hard sell. John had seen me as the boy who kept the gold spoon polished up.

I didn't want to think about John then, but I had to. His presence was palpable, something in the room behind me, something in Clem's eyes. And Clem now had time to wait, just sitting there sucking at another of Linau's cheroots. The damn thing was static time, no excuse at the moment for action at all, no reason to run out into the tropic dark and work up a good extrovert sweat. Clem did most of his sweating in his brain and maybe in his heart, too, though I couldn't be sure about that any longer. I couldn't begin to guess what the Clem behind the façade had done about his heart. I was as long a way from him as that character who had apologized to himself for using the water treatment on Lee Wat. In war you don't apologize, not if you're a real combatant.

It wasn't even comfort to know that somewhere back along the years John had faced almost exactly my present moment, something quite as precise and decisive. You go down the stairs from a sense of duty, or perhaps simply because the opportunity is there and somebody has to make the descent, and you go hearing the thin voice of reason crying in your ears, as John must have done: "You want to die? Don't come down this way, go back! Do you want to die?"

Nobody wants to die that way, but some go down. Clem had gone down, and at once became two men, the façade and the killer. John, too. I had never stopped to think how curious it was, in a world short of Johns, that someone of his abilities remained quietly in the little backwater of Bintan, a life apparently dedicated to irrigation and public works. It had never occurred to me that Bintan was an almost perfect base for an established agent, for a key man, seeming out of the world, and yet central, an inconspicuous nerve point. I had imagined my friend the old-fashioned Colonial Administrator, when in fact he was about as new-fashioned as you can get, and died because of this. Only now I remembered a sharp cynicism about the role and function of a Resident in our day, a cynicism which might have been a factor in John's decision to widen his activities.

Behind me, sucking a cheroot, sat the executioner who could, on occasion, set himself up as judge and jury, too, and not be dilatory in his multiple functions. This time he had been authorized to kill Charlie and recruit me, that is, if in his judgment, I had passed the initial tests. I didn't know whether I had passed them. I didn't really want to know.

I turned. Clem didn't lift his head to look at me.

"I think your operation stinks," I said.

"Sure."

"I believe in any kind of containment, or harassment, or even a battering trial of strength. But this isn't any of those."

"No."

"It's the kind of dirt they'd think up."

"Exactly," Clem said. "We're first this time."

"Congratulations."

His head did come up.

"Look, Paul, this war is prestige. Nothing else, really. We're losing it. Every day."

"And something like this would give you a great boost?"

"Enormous. You lure the turtle to stick out its head. Then use the chopper. China's a wily turtle."

"Where was all this cooked?"

"Right here."

"John?"

"He saw it shaping. We let it happen."

"With Charlie staked out like a goat in a clearing to lure the tiger?"

"We were talking about turtles," Clem said. "And you're giving Charlie too much importance, though he was here, and had his function. If we'd touched him the Chinks would have been warned we were onto them. So John just paid out the

[174]

rope and waited. Charlie did us a good turn, really. A useful climax to a pretty useless career."

"Enough to have earned his widow her pension?"

Clem looked straight at me.

"You could say that."

He seemed to be inviting my hatred, whipping it to a peak from which only a descent into reason and a calmer acquiescence was possible. It was as if he had seen others with my reaction, just as violent at first, others who in the end became useful in their niches. That was all he wanted, I was to be corralled into the pattern, a necessary replacement on a weak front. He couldn't really allow himself doubts about me, I was a needed recruit and his choice of potential material was very limited.

"Very much a combined operation at your level out here, isn't it?" I suggested. "A real Anglo-American alliance."

"Sure. We're just like that." Clem used his fingers. "Even though I don't like limeys."

He smiled.

Clem didn't tell me about Charlie, he didn't have to. I'd already seen it, the little man torn by his frustrations and prodded by his wife, almost inevitably set for what was to happen to him. But you couldn't even hang a decent tragedy on Charlie, he was too small for it, and the start to the finale certainly had an almost trivial beginning, just a little borrowing to help maintain the fantasy about himself, easier with Yin Tao than a bank, a friendly special arrangement that you didn't even think about a great deal until suddenly one day you found yourself held by claws and working for a new boss while still remaining in the old one's office. John had probably known about that loan the moment it was made. John knew what was coming and London knew and Charlie went on prodding the cracks in paving with his executive walking stick, needing that pith helmet which had gone out of fashion and never dreaming he was watched all the time by both sides.

[175]

Even that play about John's summons to London was a contributing factor, the threat of trouble in the Resident's career pushing the assistant just a little further out into experimental action. John had planned everything except his own death. He had slipped up there.

But I wasn't even sure on this point. There was the new will involving me which suggested the Resident had been very aware of the threat to himself.

Charlie had wept real tears for John and for his own guilt. I had come on that guilt when he suggested the Russians working with the Sultan, carefully steering away from any mention of much nearer Red neighbors. A link-up shouted from his careful avoidance of the obvious, as it had also from his irritation when I kept on bringing in Yin Tao. Charlie had the terrible transparency of the basically honest forced into deceit and frightened of an amateur incompetence in it. Even now I couldn't think of the man without recurrent spurts of sympathy, and I wondered if the watching John had felt these, too, or whether he had gone on just making those cool notes that were never entered in the official log of an administrator's journal which I had caught Charlie reading.

I didn't know the answer, I had no experience as yet of living on two levels. It was something being offered me by an old hand at the process who would be one of my instructors.

"Who shot John?" I asked, not needing the answer.

"Yin."

"Why wasn't John protected? Or more careful?"

"We were caught out. We didn't think they were nearly ready. Landing men here had been stretched out, a slow process. They only had about four hundred in the jungle. We believed they'd want to be up to battalion strength before anything broke. So John was allowed to go to the States for Lil, after consideration."

I remembered the time lag between the news of Lil's Californian performance and the departure of an angry father.

When you have gone below even your domestic life is controlled by policy.

"You had checks on exactly what the Chinese were up to?"

"Look, Paul, we knew when those junks left Hainan and what their load was. We let them through the U.S. Pacific fleet. The whole business could have been stopped at any time and would have been if we'd thought for one moment we were losing control."

"But you did lose it when John went to America and Linau was suddenly called to Hong Kong for a conference with her Red bosses?"

"You could say that."

"How long have you had Linau?"

"All of three years."

"John did the persuading? In bed?"

"We leave details of that kind to the man on the spot."

"It's nice to know you allow your people a personal life."

Clem smiled again.

"So long as it doesn't become obtrusive."

I'd guessed at Linau's picture before I had the whole one, the Royal playgirl out in the world and being heavily bid for by the Russians who were just longing for a Far Eastern toe hold. She had played with them because she was thinking of little Bintan with its oil and ruled by her own family gone soft. Her state, to survive, and to remain an el Badas province, needed a strong hand who had real experience in the great contemporary game of juggling the bids for assistance from the world's powerful people. You can even maintain a political anachronism like Bintan if you become a really trained juggler. And Linau had signed on for the course, first with the Russians, afterward with Peking. Then John came into it, persuading her that the West wasn't quite a spent force. She took on a new role with instructions to penetrate as deeply as possible into Mao's plans for her little country and report back. I asked how successful the Princess had been.

[177]

Clem stared at his cheroot.

"It looked all right. But Yin's been the problem. Local party boss naturally resented Linau, quite aside from the fact that he didn't have any reason to love the el Badas family. One of the things we have to be thankful for is the time the Reds spend watching each other. It's held up their take-over bid for the world. Yin has worked hard trying to stymie Linau with Peking. He even flew up there to cook her goose. But she was ready for that and had already confessed her liaison with John, which was Yin's big bomb. That went fizz. Linau had been told to go on sleeping with hated colonialist and listening to anything he said between snores. Maybe Peking had got hold of one of those old Mata Hari pictures. Or just been charmed by the lady. She can be very charming. At any rate we were counting on that. But may have been wrong."

"Why?"

"Yin's totally in control here now, and couldn't be without Peking's approval. The trip to Hong Kong was a blind. Linau has been shut right out of what's happening, from the moment she landed off your launch. She's had the not-surprising feeling that she was probably under sentence of death. Just like you and me."

"You?"

"Oh, sure. Yin's wise to me all right. It was no time for a color-photography enthusiast to land. I think it's highly probable that the trained soldier who nearly got you at the rest house was really meant to get me. Every white man looks the same to a Chink, remember. And Yin would have been doing a bit of thinking about last night. He could scarcely expect you to be responsible for all that activity in the dark, especially when he knew that you'd brought Lee Wat back for quite a strenuous session."

"How did he know that?"

"We found Lee Wat behind one of the servants' empty

houses. Just pulled back into the bushes. With his throat cut. He probably talked before he got it."

Teacher had already started. Lesson one was that you don't go soft after administering the water torture. I remembered then Clem admonishing me gently for being a rough boy. That was a laugh.

I sat down. I've never felt more the amateur out of his depth than in those moments. It was the depths which were unnerving, the elaborate patterns down there and the quietness in which most of them were worked out. I was very conscious of Clem's quietness now, the man who knows he has reached the moments for waiting and is composed in them whatever may be happening beyond.

The build-up for Operation Turtle had started from an incident at sea which didn't really seem to point toward Bintan at all. A North Borneo opium-patrol launch had given chase to a junk which didn't stop for search but instead went beetling off at an all-out fifteen knots which suggested to me—though I kept quiet about this to Clem—that the thing was equipped with one of my Dolphin engines. The junk made for a pattern of small islands off the Bintanese coast but didn't manage an escape this way. The crew, seeing they were going to be boarded, did something rather unusual for Chinese, who are conservative about abandoning any kind of property; they attempted to scuttle their junk, then swam for it to an island. The patrol skipper got on board quickly enough to close the bungs opened in her bilges, keeping the craft afloat and taking it in tow. He didn't bother about the crew, wisely, for the islands were thick jungle.

The junk's cargo was extremely interesting, conventional with copra on the surface, highly unconventional with a ton's worth of small arms underneath, complete with ammo, and—most interesting of all—four crated five-inch mortars of a new design incorporating Oriental ingenuity of a kind that would give no comfort to people who still think the Eastern races fifty years behind the West in technical know-how. A mortar is, after all, a small cannon, not the sort of thing normally supplied to local partisans of Red Chinese democracy, for it isn't really a handy guerrilla weapon. The fact that this junk was caught near Bintan could have been chance, but John didn't think so, and no one could quite understand why there should be any secret supply line to Indonesians over in East Borneo involving a use of this west coast. There was no need, either, for Chinese to be secretive about shipments to their allies.

John came up with the take-over-in-Bintan theory and nobody laughed at him. Intelligence was put to work from outside el Badas's little state, and very efficiently. Jungle and coast watchers from southern Sarawak were on hand to report, all of two months after the capture of the junk, the first arrival in Bintan of Chinese irregulars, fully equipped and wearing jungle-green camouflage, but no insignia. Their junks were fast and came at night almost certainly with my engines driving them, part of a package deal with Peking for a thousand Dolphins which now began to feel a highly immoral piece of legitimate trade, though Clem didn't even hint at this angle or suggest that a brand name stamped on a hunk of metal had been a starting point for some investigations into my political allegiances.

The first Chinese units went straight into the jungle, deep in, establishing base camps to which further rivals, at spaced intervals, were conducted by local guides in on the revolution. To avoid the giveaway of marked porterage trails the junks landed at different points along Bintan's coastline, though they did make considerable steady use of one small village, entirely occupied by *hua-chiao* rice growers, which was two miles up a small river, offering good anchorage and a jetty for unloading heavier supplies.

When John was allowed to go to America there were four

hundred irregulars in Bintan and from supplies landed the clear indications were a build-up to battalion strength at least before the local D day. The landing rate of men put this day months ahead and our plane crash in Malaya hadn't caused real alarm because John was fairly certain it had been designed for me. His killing had found Operation Turtle plotted, but not at any readiness alert.

I wasn't flattered by the thought that Charlie had been allowed to send for me simply because the idea of my presence in Bintan caused no increase in Yin's blood pressure. Also, it was important that a normal surface be kept on the local patterns until the very last moment. But my contact with Linau en route, reported from Singapore airport, must have made Yin think again, and fast, since the Princess was by that time under sentence from Peking and might easily have guessed this and be wanting help. Yin had thought it wisest to eliminate the unknown factor, threat or not, and had arranged for the plastic bomb.

It was a busy morning for him. Linau hadn't been home ten minutes when Yin phoned, a call he enjoyed making, as though he had been waiting for this moment for some years. The Princess was not to try to get to her brother at the palace. If she did she would be shot down. She was also to avoid the Residency radio. All her movements were being watched. Yin had suggested extreme discretion as her only possible policy. When he hung up Linau at once tried to ring her brother but the call hadn't even been put through. She tested the lead on her by coming to the rest house to offer me hospitality and got away with that, though her mission hadn't been basically humane at all. It occurred to her that me under her roof just might be a card to use against Yin. She didn't get a chance to use that card and was so spared inevitable disillusionment. It was clear that Yin didn't give a damn about Linau since he had her on Peking's out-list.

Clem, sitting opposite me, was back at a curiously disconcerting habit of staring at his toecaps, rather as though they were twin crystal balls.

"Did you come here to rescue Linau?" I asked.

He shook his head.

"We don't go in for chivalry. It's too expensive in personnel."

"So it was to check up on me?"

"Yes, friend."

"What the hell did you think I might be doing?"

"Anything at all. The odor of your reputation has traveled quite a distance."

"But for me you'd have kept away to let the boil burst?"

"You put it nicely."

"And you're ready now to deal with Yin's coup?"

"That's my pious hope. According to plan, thirty minutes after the el Badas freedom-for-Bintan broadcast down comes the chopper. There's a British carrier which ought now to be traveling north at speed, with its planes right up on deck. You'll appreciate that this has to be a totally British action? To abide by international law, to which we all make our salaams." He smiled. "Everything is going to drop right on the Reds here, wham. They're counting on a day or two of nice muddle before we take action, too late as usual, which they can use to establish themselves. And the so-legitimate-looking new regime. But they're not getting the muddle this time. We'll have them copped. Doing exactly what Mao has said recently they never intend to do and we all know he's a liar. That is, moving into aggression abroad with their own troops. We think the whole of Asia is going to be just terribly interested in Bintan. Both in what China was up to here and in our swift reaction to it. Our remarkably speedy reaction."

"The biggest morale boost in these parts for a decade?"

"You're right with it," Clem said. "The Red defeat in Malaya was too long and drawn out to have much drama value. But this is superb theater."

"Provided Yin hasn't been scared off the whole idea by your arrival."

"I'm not that important. And I've minimized that factor by moving in here as one of the defeated party. It looks like surrender. It is, in fact, a surrender of sorts. I'm immobilized. The next move is Yin's."

"Why did you want to use the Residency radio?"

"To send a message in clear for Yin's boys to monitor. Making it plain that I'm an agent, which Yin knows, but also showing clearly that I'm clueless as to what's up."

"You think Yin would have swallowed that?"

"It's my experience that even very smart people tend to believe what suits their plans. And it was worth trying. Incidentally, I was not Charlie's executioner. He shot at the radio first all right, but that was only because he couldn't see the Luger I'd put on a shelf. He was moving his gun to me next when I got him. Just in the act, you might say. Does that put my halo right back where it ought to be?"

"Practically makes you a Rover Scout. Clem, just what was Charlie up to in these last days? Did he have a role?"

"I don't think so. He'd exhausted his usefulness to them and to us. And I guess he realized that. It made him wander around those empty corridors trying to find himself. Only there was nothing to find."

"Did he hear you breaking in?"

"Must have done. I made some noises over the shutters to the study. They were locked. I think he probably stood outside that door listening. And waiting. Anyway, he opened it like someone who had been taking his time, slowly. His last orders were that the set wasn't to be used. So he acted on them."

"He kept trotting to see el Badas at the palace?"

"His Highness needs an audience all the time. It's an affliction of the great. And the people he usually manages to keep around him have been a bit occupied recently."

I got up.

"How do you get service in this place? And where's our hostess?"

"Probably burning secret documents as they do in beleaguered embassies. We haven't got around yet to training our lady operatives to eat up their files."

"Do you trust her, Clem?"

"About as much as I'd trust you. But the girl's in a spot all right. Yin's taking over her kingdom, the one she used to run with a puppet. And it gives her no future."

It occurred to me that Clem's thirty minutes between the el Badas broadcast and the chopper coming down was probably the usual underestimate of delay factors for which enough allowance is never made at executive level. Two hours or three was more likely, during which time Yin would be quite busy establishing his new order but not overworked to the point of forgetting all about a houseful of undesirable reactionaries entirely at his mercy. The extrovert in me, never very deeply submerged, suggested an armed resistance which would at least given us a chance. I put this up to Clem.

"It appears the Princess now only really trusts five of her servants," he said. "And I think that's an optimistic estimate. The poor girl's been badly disillusioned."

"How many are there altogether?"

"Seventeen, including the cook."

"Couldn't we push twelve of them out the gate?"

"I doubt if we'd live to complete the operation. But even if we did it wouldn't do us a lot of good. Part of Linau's disillusionment is the fact that someone has removed all small arms from their usual caches about this residence. Apparently she had quite an armory, not believing entirely in brains alone. I have this Luger making a bulge in my pocket, with four bullets left. That's not a lot to hold off China. Or even twelve servants."

"What the hell do we do? Sit here?"

"Yes. No one's pinched the whisky."

I walked away from Clem. He was a depressive influence. I went to a door under the erotic mural and opened it. There was no hint of the man with the parang about which American intelligence had warned me, just an empty passage. This appeared to lead to a guest wing and struck a note of austerity after the owner's quarters, as though it were a later edition executed by a Singapore contractor who had got the word about contemporary building for the tropics, where you seal out the sun with small windows high up and then use strip lighting to illumine the gloom created. There were even plastic tiles on the floor.

One door was open and I looked in. It appeared to be a workroom, with a desk and steel filing cabinets. The place was empty and tidy. I then heard music and went toward it; not Boots this time, classic jazz. Lil had pinched back the record player Clem hadn't used.

She was sitting on the floor in what looked like a university residence cell, everything built in, convenient and hygienic, and from the taste of the air artificially cooled. The music wasn't Lil's, but it was a noise, filling time and space and somehow giving her total immunity to present circumstance.

"Hello," she said. "You've lost your bandages. And you don't look like the King of Siam any more."

"Did I ever?"

"In that bed."

She giggled.

"Lil, you seem to have influence around here. Could you get me trousers? Or shorts? And the extra luxury of a shirt would be appreciated."

"Where from?" She flicked off the player. "There are no resident males."

"The servants?"

Lil's eyes, painted again to help put in the time, squinted at me.

"I might get a fit from the cook. He's big for a Chinese."

"You know how to find him?"

"Of course. I've been like a little dog running around, sniffing at all the strange corners." She got up. "All right, I'll try."

"While you're at it could you locate my hostess? I'd like to drop a hint that I'm hungry."

"Linau's gone."

"She's . . . what?"

"If you're hungry I could get the cook to make something."

"Lil, do you mean Linau's not in this house?"

"I'm sure she's not. I heard a car drive off."

"When?"

"Let me think. About half an hour ago, maybe."

"You know where she's gone?"

"No. Linau just does things. She doesn't talk about doing them."

My breathing seemed to tighten. I went back to Clem, to shake his remarkable composure just a little. My news made him sit up but there was no wild bounce onto his feet.

"It could be a top-level conference," I said. "Peking having changed its mind about a Princess. There's a phone in her study."

"Yin wouldn't change his mind. Not even under pressure. He's boss here."

"Then she's made a bolt for it?"

"Where to? The road ends in jungle. It's a long walk to Sarawak."

"You gave me the impression of this house surrounded by guards."

"No, Paul, the guards were all established inside. And had been for long enough. If she went she's been allowed to go."

It was nice then to see Clem without an answer, really deeply and profoundly restoring to my humbled and battered spirit to be a witness in these moments when he hadn't a thing

to dish up on a tray and offer with an almost Oriental politeness. Instead of three enemies of a people's democracy waiting
for execution there were now only two. I didn't include Lil
because I couldn't see even the Reds shooting anyone so profoundly out of touch with her environment. She'd still be
playing classic jazz when a firing squad put Clem and me up
against a courtyard wall. That girl had a natural immunity to
real pain and stress which might well turn out to be the only
asset she required to take her safely through life. It was a factor which indicated a re-think of the Boots Kinsley relation if
I got out of this corner and was able to face up to what now
seemed a decidedly minor duty and responsibility.

"My God!" Clem said.

He was looking out toward the balcony. I turned to see that
it wasn't night any more, but dawn seven hours early. We
reached the railing at the same moment, leaning on it, staring.

The parachute flare had come down from a great height and
switched itself on over Bintan town, like a hand torch from
the Almighty, sepulchral whiteness in a vast vault of night,
and we were revealed in its probing glare, detail of town and
trees and buildings all given a sharp clarity that sun haze
blurred. It was almost as though the next development was
certain to be a monster trumpet blast from the heavens telling
man that it was finally too late to repent. I felt suddenly almost cold out there, as though the light had brought its own
chill. And I had a sense of events suddenly beyond my puny
twitchings at the edge of them.

From the look on Clem's face he was feeling the same way.

"They didn't wait," he said after a moment, and with deep
bitterness.

I saw what he meant. Into the lasting radius of brightness,
but from above it, came the pallid, gently rolling mushrooms
of descending parachutes, hundreds of them.

"I didn't hear plane engines," Clem said, with a kind of
anger. "Did you?"

[187]

"No."

All I'd heard was classic jazz.

"They must have been damn high!"

"And the war's on," I said.

"It's over. Look at the town."

Bintan, under the light from heaven, had all the quiet innocence of Eden before the fall, a little oasis of stillness in a rowdy world which couldn't even be quickly startled awake because all its sleepers were enjoying the rest given to clear consciences. A few lights came on, red against whiteness, but even these without haste, and the total stillness wasn't broken. No one jumped in a car for a quick getaway from the unknown, not even a dog barked. And then we did get a protest, from a rooster.

The mushrooms wobbled slightly in heat thermals, within range of fire from the ground now, but there was no crack of a rifle. Bintan was waking to rub its eyes, astonished but not really apprehensive. I saw a man suspended from the chute nearest us, quite clearly, and he had an automatic gun pointing down, as though ready to use it while still airborne.

"They're making for the Residency grounds!"

"Yes," Clem said. "That and the palace. They're sticking to plan. A few hours too soon. Damn and damn! And they'll be landing at the oil company, too. Can't you just see a hastily organized reception out there? Getting out the gin bottles. Always throw a party for the military, our shield in trouble, even when there's no trouble."

"Hey!" I said.

"What?"

"Chinese firecrackers. Long ago. Yin's withdrawal signal."

"Could be. It doesn't matter what the signal was. Why the hell couldn't they have waited for that broadcast?"

"Worried about you?"

"Shut up, damn you!"

"Linau knew the signal. She knew what firecrackers meant. Did she tell you about them?"

"You know damn well the bitch didn't."

"She's with her brother now. Holding his hand. Want to bet?"

"I want that whisky bottle," Clem said.

Back in the sitting room he didn't look like a man who has just had a reprieve from liquidation. He looked smitten with sharp personal grief. Operation Turtle, now dead, had been his baby.

"We'll chase 'em into the jungle," he said. "We know where those camps are."

"You'll find clearings. Nothing else."

"What the hell do you mean?"

"Remember the *History of Sarawak* you took to bed with you? When Raja Brooke made a comeback his Dyaks killed a lot of Chinese, but a lot of them got away into jungle. Some hundreds. They just disappeared. The jungle is as much the mother of fugitives today as it was then."

"What's all that light?" Lil was standing directly under that Chinese party holding clothes for me. "There's something funny going on around here. I can't find the cook. Or any of the servants."

The servants had fled from the wrath to come, the fury of a Dyak princess who was scarcely likely to become celebrated for clemency toward traitors within her own gates. I had a feeling that Linau, probably with a strict publicity censorship for the sake of her international reputation, was still going to be an avenger of the kind who passes into legend and is eventually sung about when you want a number to really give you the creeps. Authentic folk music about rows of pickled heads a-swinging from hair on a washing line.

"I'll take those trousers, Lil. Thanks for pinching them."

"Paul, what *is* happening?"

"We've been rescued."

"From what?"

It was going to take a long time to tell her.

"Does Linau have more than one car?"

"Yes, three. A Jag and a Daimler and a sports Triumph."

A nice civilized selection for your mood of the moment. The two big cars had been left and we took the Daimler, a more dignified vehicle for an approach to the Royal Presence. Before I got it out of the garage the second flare died away and there was no follow-up, none needed. The paratroops were all down and not a shot had been fired.

ELEVEN

SPLIT-SECOND timing, that ideal of all military operations, isn't achieved as often as the writers of popular war histories tend to suggest. There is always the acute danger of someone jumping the gun somewhere and starting off a chain reaction which reduces the element of surprise to a remarkable minimum.

I drove the Daimler thinking about ways that Yin might have been warned. It could have come from Clem's arrival in Bintan, which rather meant that I was personally responsible for the whole debacle simply because I had been recognized by a princess in an airport lounge, bought her whisky, and then by my chat on a plane made her decide to shout for help. Quite naturally, however, I preferred the view that the coming official enquiries would absolve me, switching blame to some careless talk before a very large aircraft carrier sailed out of Singapore for an undisclosed destination at a time when no exercises were on schedule, the same carrier seen steaming north at speed by a junk which reported in to alert high-flying Chinese spotter planes from Hainan. Operation Turtle had been up against pretty heavy odds even before I started blundering about at the edges of it, but I couldn't feel that Clem had come to see this yet. He sat beside me, hunched over, sending out radiations of dislike which ought to have chilled me to the marrow but really had the reverse effect. For after all this I couldn't see him carrying on with any idea about recruiting me for undercover work, however great his need. There are some people—unscientific as this may sound—

who have a curious flare for attracting disaster to the organizations they serve. I believed now that I was out before I had been in, bounced back to my adolescent games which suddenly seemed vastly attractive and no longer a cause for shame at all.

"Sometime, somewhere, someone's going to tell me what this is all about," Lil said from the back seat.

I promised to do it, then turned the car into the road leading past the Residency. This was all lit up, as though an army was in there looking for something, most probably the enemy. The town, too, which we had to pass through to get to the palace, was awake, but there were no paratroopers in the streets, just a large portion of the populace informally dressed to the point of near nakedness, all curious but none of them looking in the least frightened. They were just the audience at a vast pageant, arranged for them at great expense and trouble, a bit unhappy about having missed most of the spectacular opening number due to bad timing on the part of the producers. I had to drive very slowly, and we created some interest as though we might turn out to be a minor comic number mildly worth watching. We got stares and heard laughter all around, but there was no hint of any hostility. Food stalls had opened to cater for an unexpected trade and the smell of acetylene mixed with an aromatic smoke from barbecuing slabs of water buffalo. Dogs ran around wagging tails.

None of this prepared us for what happened halfway along the shore road to the palace. I had put on a little speed, but not much, for fear of bicycles coming without lamps out of lanes, when our own lights were blotted out in a hard-white glare suggesting another flare. I was braking hard when there was one shot, the first of the war, and this apparently not in anger, just a message. This was followed almost at once by a Sandhurst military-college voice on a loud hailer telling us to advance in low gear and be recognized.

Clem under all this publicity wasn't looking happy. The top security man is at a sharp disadvantage when it comes to dealing with the regular services. He can't reveal anything about himself, even to high-level brass, and has to pass as a civilian at a time when this isn't much of a status.

"What are we?" I asked.

"Refugees."

"From what?"

"That damn rest house."

He had something there.

The terrible mechanized voice bellowed at us again.

"Stop! Get out of the car with your hands over your head!"

There have been other occasions in my life when I've met up like this, almost casually, with the official forces working for the cause I believed I'd been serving and my receptions have always been memorably cold. I climbed out on the road, lifting my arms, very conscious of what I'd been through recently for democracy in Bintan, thinking that the fairly active man in the trouble areas of our age is always being threatened by that final irony of getting a well-aimed bullet from his own side.

I'd thought Lil's presence would result in an immediate relaxation of security, but it didn't, apparently because the girl hadn't put her arms up and couldn't see any reason why she should.

"Hands over head, woman!"

Lil had certainly wanted to grow up quickly, but she took a moment or two to react to an order giving her this maturity. Then her expression changed from one of sheer enjoyment of her evening to a badly controlled fury. Two paws went up, somewhat, reaching about shoulder level. We still hadn't seen the slightest sign of human movement in the glare area.

"Clem," I whispered. "You didn't bring that Luger along? We'll be arrested as fifth columnists."

"I'm not nuts. It's at Linau's."

Figures came into light, first a man in a tin hat who looked far too young to be a captain, but with a face hardened by experience in a part of the world for which he clearly had little affection. His person was strung about with lethal weapons, ammo belts, grenade pouches, and there was an automatic rifle in his hands, held up. Behind him were two more figures similarly equipped. We were frisked, with no particular courtesies for the lady, before there was any real human contact which never became in the least warm. The car behind us searched and only then did the captain take a deep breath, to be brusque.

"What do you want here?"

"To see your colonel," I said.

"My daddy was the Resident," Lil announced. "He was murdered. We thought we were going to be."

In her own way the girl was catching up with contemporary history, bright enough to make sharp deductions. The captain stared at her. Their years weren't far apart but he didn't look like a Bangers fan at all. Pop stars could zoom to the heavens and plunge again during a young soldier's tour of Eastern service and it was quite likely that, as with so many before him, he had become enthusiastic about the entertainment potential of the nubile local girls. These are one of the compensations for the discomforts of the Orient, the worse the posting, the better-looking the girls, a kind of natural law which allows a man something to live for he doesn't mention in letters home. Lil's Occidental plumpness clearly didn't appeal at all to this boy and after just a moment she felt this, sharply. The white light showed color change in her face.

They made us leave the car and walk under escort and we only achieved a very slow progress through bristling defense perimeters, but once in the palace all this alertness disappeared. Inside was spacious emptiness, no sign of native servants or royal guard, not even the fans working, the place like an administrative block in New Delhi in the days of the British

[194]

raj, but during the monsoon season, when everyone stopped administrating India and went to the hills for a season of sex games. There was an army clerk already at work in one corner and already bored, somehow looking as though he had been dropped from the heavens all in one piece along with desk, field telephone, In and Out trays, and a suitcase full of forms in triplicate. He glanced at us but decided that if we'd got this far he couldn't stop us, so bent his head again, another male ignoring Lil. I began to feel for her.

We went three abreast down a vaulted corridor toward what I remembered had been a kind of audience hall, the official center of palace life, where el Badas had a carved chair with rubies stuck in it, rather hinting at the throne to which he wasn't actually entitled. At this stage there was no sound to guide us but it was somewhere to go and I like the purposeful approach. Mirrors at intervals showed me how I looked in a cook's trousers, which ended two inches up my shinbones, and in his best shirt. They also showed me that I needed a shave. Lil was doing things with her fingers to her hair, angrily. Clem was staring at the tiles and not putting his feet on the lines between them.

One half of a double door just ahead opened enough to let out the noise of a man shouting and then shut again to cut this off. The major standing there was in battle dress like everyone else but the way he wore it said plainly that at the first possible moment he would get himself starched up.

"Looking for someone?" It was a polite enquiry and surprising.

Clem had lapsed into the half-gloomy silences of a Midwestern boy suddenly plopped down into the middle of an unlimited number of British. He looked rather as though all his background made him very reluctant to admit that hordes of these oddities, who shared his language up to a point, were still about.

"We'd like to see your colonel," I said again.

"I see. Well, the old man seems to be fighting a political battle at the moment and he's not frightfully good at them. You heard the noise? Actually, it might be best to wait. Unless, of course, you're local admin chaps and might help?"

He looked at my trousers and decided that this could never be. He looked at Clem and was vaguely troubled.

"We've been staying with the Princess," I said.

His eyes widened.

"Really? That must have been a bit of luck for you. She's quite a piece, isn't she? And in that case you might be useful. Just go in and stand at the back somewhere. I've got to get the war moving again."

We went in and stood at the back. It was a room that could have been the ballroom annex of a large hotel, but the kind of hotel in which trade had begun to fall off at the end of the twenties. The decor was mighty Wurlitzer, in the Tom Mix movie-house tradition, chandeliers, carved plaster, vast dust-trap drapes on huge rounded windows and over all a powerful, pervading smell of warmed plush. At one end, where the band should have been, was Linau, seated on the mock throne, wearing a gold court sarong and diamonds, and surrounded by so many relations it all looked rather like a tableau photograph of the late German Emperor at one of his many house parties, nearly swamped by Hohenzollerns. This was the royal family of Bintan, the male side of it, about seventy strong and to a man pensioners of the oil company, each long used to a life on a totally unearned income. Everyone was there, a gaggle of Tunkups, except el Badas whose corpulent absence was at once highly conspicuous, at least to me.

In front of the rulers stood four British soldiers in uniforms decidedly mussed up from rough parachute landings, one of them clearly the colonel. He was a thin, almost small man in his early fifties with the sort of complexion which seems to be the result of too many quick changes of climate, rather mottled. He had seen a lot of the dying which only rates a by-line on the third inside page of big newspapers and his recent wars had all been the minor ones that people at home forget about before they are quite over. Because Linau stopped speaking to look at us the colonel turned and looked at us, too. I wouldn't have liked him for an enemy.

"Who the hell let you in here?"

It wasn't a gentle question. Linau answered for us, and with flat authority.

"They're my guests. They can stay."

"Now look here, Madame . . ."

"Princess," she corrected.

For a moment there was total silence between them, then the Colonel avoided this little issue.

"I am the officer commanding British forces sent to Bintan to re-establish order."

"Which has never really been disturbed."

"So you say!"

"Yes, Colonel. We have had certain difficulties which have been resolved. Your force is not necessary."

"I demand to see His Highness the Sultan!"

"And I have told you that this is quite impossible. My brother is seriously ill. At the moment he is unconscious."

"I still demand to see him!"

Linau moved slightly in the high-backed chair.

"Colonel, you are speaking to the Regent of Bintan. Duly appointed by my brother's Privy Council."

That was a meeting behind closed doors I'd have enjoyed attending when Linau, and not for the first time, asserted her authority over the el Badas tribe, bringing them swiftly to heel by a reminder that only a united front without the slightest crack in it could preserve the Royal incomes intact. I didn't have the slightest doubt that the Sultan was at this moment totally unconscious, having been persuaded it was the only expedient thing to be by a sister waving a hypodermic needle.

It's not every day that a British colonel comes bang up against a newly appointed Regent and there's absolutely nothing in the *Manual for Officers* about how to deal with this situation. It was something for the political chaps who had once again delayed their arrival until the army had established a big enough control area to allow them room in which to operate effectively.

"What about Chinks in Bintan? Irregulars?" the colonel asked loudly. "Are you saying that there aren't any?"

"There have been some lawless elements. And their contacts in the town. These have now been dealt with."

"Dealt with? Who by?"

"Me," Linau said. "I have put a price on certain heads."

Somehow she made it clear that she expected to see the heads, too. I had to hand it to her then; the air of authority wasn't new, but something more had been added, a dignity which quickly descends as a gift on those who have moved into the seats of power. Hers was a very large family, only fractionally worth anything, and she was the fraction. In many ways I'm in favor of the hereditary principle in government, with one proviso, and this is that there is no direct line by precedence of birth which automatically elevates. Ruling families can be justified provided they are flexible enough in themselves to chuck out an heir if it becomes plain that he is never going to make a good boss. After all, contemporary capitalism functions to a large degree on this basis, of families controlling corporations, and trained to do it, and holding on for a long time, too, but they only manage this by competitive selection among the top candidates. The alternative to a highly adaptable top echelon is the take-over by another family which has kept its business blood lines activated. Linau, the throwback to extrovert aggression, was the local candidate for the hour, and the only one.

Women are moving out into government in other Eastern areas, still with a tendency toward the unconventional, like putting bombs in rivals' limousines, but for all this learning the ropes of power and giving it an interesting feminine twist in some cases. With Linau as Regent I didn't see a great deal of hope for any union of Bintan with Federated Malaysia unless she could be persuaded that this would be greatly to her own advantage and her state's, but on the credit side was the fact that no Red would ever get into the place again by any back door while this Princess was watching. A Communist is just as disturbed by the thought of having his head pickled as any citizen of a freedom-loving democracy. And it was my bet that the word would go round behind iron and bamboo curtains to lay off certain free-enterprise oil wells.

In due course it might even be possible to sell Linau the idea of basic social reforms. I wasn't deeply impressed by her essential humanity, but on the other hand she had been out in the larger world a great deal, tasting both Communism and its more agreeable alternative and she must realize by now that controlled change is inevitable and a little nontribal selflessness a useful political weapon.

With these thoughts I looked at those princes massed around a woman in a chair, descendants of active men but themselves about as socially effective as vegetables. Some of them, in youth, were still quite pretty, but all over thirty-five bore the clear physical marks of too much good living in a warm climate. The total of their achievement and at the same time their only source of unease in the world, was a high output of little el Badases which brought with it the usual parental problems about careers for offspring, or rather the avoidance of anything resembling a career. The existing pensions were being stretched by a rapid natural increase and a bigger dividend rate had been an obsession which had brought them all, as a dynasty, very near the brink of disaster. This much they saw clearly, and sweat was jeweling their dusky brows.

I think that in these moments Clem was busy considering the matter of women operatives in the spy business and was about ready to issue a ruling eliminating them in future at all levels, at least in the Orient. It is never easy at any time to assess the true motivations of a double agent, and when this agent is a woman her plans for a personal destiny are even more obscure. The irritating thing about Linau's case was probably that her motivations had in a way been obvious all along, she wanted to do more effectively what she had in many respects done for years, run the country.

But for Yin the Princess would never have been anybody's agent. The Chinese merchant had, however, started to function in Bintan with the tremendous power of Peking behind him, gradually gaining an ascendancy over a fat playboy, while the sister's star was threatened with eclipse. To fight Yin Linau had first become a Red herself and then gone White over Red with John, luring her brother on to the kind of folly which would topple him but establish her. She saw clearly the risks in what was being attempted, for if the Reds won that was the end of all el Badases in Bintan, something she could probably have explained to her brother if she had been really trying, but it became policy not to. Linau had also seen that the failure of Operation Turtle ending in Yin's defeat and flight would be a splendid opportunity for her to seize power, that is if she moved quickly the moment there was the withdrawal signal. And she had moved very quickly.

I couldn't see much of a future for Abdul el Badas. It didn't seem likely that he would be permanently kept under drugs, or have his soup poisoned, but I felt that his active days were over, and that a permanent decline in his physical condition, watched over in sweetness by a loving sister, would involve his virtual retirement from public life. We were already in the throne room of a queen, and all that was left for her was to alter its decor somewhat, which I was sure she would do.

Even the colonel, clearly no convinced royalist except for British monarchs, was beginning to be worn down by Linau's composed control. We listened, protests dying away, with only a mental muttering from Clem, to a new Oriental despot in the making who used American nail polish and French scent together with a lot of phrases which have become the verbal coin in international chit-chat, such as "inviolable national integrity" and "self-determination of a free people." Some of these had just a faintly Marxist tinge still, something to expect really from her mixed conditioning and fairly certain to be quickly polished away. She was talking about her plans for restoring complete and total order when Manson's name came into it as her doughty upholder of the law. This came to me with quite a jerk for it seemed only too possible that Linau mightn't now have a chief of police at all.

Neither Clem nor Lil noticed me leaving, the one sunk in total reorganization after disaster, the other drawing up a charter for a Princess Linau fan club. Outside the palace I found the army in the process of moving from a secured position into the town and they wouldn't let me go on ahead, turning me into an unwilling attachment to rear H.Q. advancing and it was nearly two hours before I was able to shake myself free of a peaceful occupation of totally cheerful streets from which the populace were gradually going back to bed. Alone I walked up a hill toward the police station where the flag of Bintan, green and yellow stripes with a tiny Union Jack in one corner, was still flying on a white flagstaff. The building was of two stories, with many of the windows to the front lit, but the jail annex at the back dark and gloomy. I walked over a courtyard laid with whitewashed stones and up into a hall where my feet made a noise on boards. The place should have been a scene of some bustle, but was deathly quiet. Doors stood open. Not a soul moved in the passages. I felt like calling out: "Anybody home?"

There was someone home. He was at a desk in a large office where an air conditioner hummed, a man slumped forward on his arms from a cane-backed chair, only clipped hair showing, the face buried. I stood there almost on tiptoe looking for signs of blood and not seeing any signs of breathing. Then the head jerked up. A face turned to me, the pock-marked thug's face of Manson's quisling chief sergeant.

I had no gun. His was on the desk in front of him, very near his fingers. He stared at me, eyes very bloodshot.

"Tuan," he said like a child, in a very small voice.

The phone on the desk began to ring, loud in a building empty of people and with doors open. It didn't galvanize the sergeant into any sudden activity. He shook his head to clear some fogging there, then slowly pushed out his hand to the receiver, brushing past the gun as he did so. It interested me that the exchange was active again after having been so aggressively dormant. The operators must have only recently faced up to their moments of decision, whether to bolt for it or to bluff out their roles under Yin, counting on an almost irreplaceable importance in a backyard country as trained technicians. Obviously they had decided on the bluff, and the line sounded a good one though the English coming at him seemed too much for the sergeant. He used a little Malay, choked on it, and put the receiver down. I walked over and picked it up.

"Hello, hello?" I knew the voice at once. "This is the Singapore police. Inspector Kang."

"Nice to hear you, old friend."

"Eh?"

"Harris at this end, ready to take your message."

"So the Bintan police have got you where I never could? What are you, a trusty?"

"I'm in charge, it looks like."

"Really?" said Kang in his graceful manner. "It was Manson I was hoping to have a word with. Offering him any help he might need."

"He's out. But I'll tell him."

"Do. Suggest he get in touch with me at once, please. Your man Ohashi has kept ringing me up. About fifteen times in twenty-four hours. He was worried."

"You didn't pass on his fears to anyone?"

"I'm abnormally discreet. Why?"

The sergeant had put his hands over his face and appeared to be massaging his nose.

"Kang, someone's mucked up one of the cleverest come-ons in years."

"And you're trying to convince yourself it wasn't you? Have lunch with me on the way home. The police can also act as confessors, you know. There is something about telling all to a policeman which is likely to send an operator at the edge of the law like you rejoicing on his way. I take it you are coming home?"

"As soon as I can. Look, could you ring Ohashi for me?"

"It'll be a pleasure, Mr. Harris. So the Linau woman is now Regent?"

I was astonished.

"How could you know so soon?"

"The radio. Princess Linau addressed the world while British troops were floating down on her brother's palace. You didn't hear it?"

"No."

"I see. Well, it was a very moving speech, if you're easily affected by oratory from the heart. She told us about her brother's illness which oddly none of us had heard of here even though we were listening very hard to any noises from Bintan. This illness had forced her to assume high office as Regent at the request of her family. Actually she implied the family was devoted to her. Which was news also. Then she ended on a very beautiful note about being willing to give the last drop of her blood for Bintan."

"Everyone else's last drop," I said.

"So that's your impression of the lady? Mine, too, Still, she's a definite personality."

"You could say that."

"And Bintan certainly needs one. Well, I won't keep you from administering the local police in an emergency. Is Manson at the palace?"

"I'm not quite sure."

"He's not dead by any chance?"

"I don't know yet."

"Well, find out and ring me back, will you? It will put me slightly in your debt which ought to be handy for you in the future. I'm expecting to spend the rest of the night in this office."

"Were you expecting to have to rush in a contingent of your police to assist the military here?"

"It had occurred to me as a possibility."

"And would give you a nice toe hold in Bintan, wouldn't it?"

"You're such a suspicious character, Harris."

Contact with Singapore, and especially with Kang, was heartening, giving me strength to deal with the curious problem of an emotionally disturbed sergeant of the police. The man seemed almost grateful that I had appeared to take over. He raised a sin- and grief-ravaged face to say, in Malay:

"I'm a criminal."

It isn't often you run into people so willing to confirm your assessment of them. It's rather endearing. He looked to me like a strong, fairly wicked man who needed a good cry to get the tensions out of his system. Most Oriental males, that is, in the warmer areas, cry very easily and this has resulted not surprisingly, and despite disturbed political conditions, in a remarkably low need for psychiatric treatment. Nations in which males weep, even under minor provocation, and with

[204]

drama in public when the occasion demands it, may not produce the best soldiers but they do turn out wonderful husbands and lovers. And a bit of top-level executive bawling in New York, London, Tokyo and Hamburg would certainly go a long way toward bringing down the ulcer rate, and probably coronaries as well. It might even improve business efficiency once the new behavior pattern was established.

I was quite happy when tears came to the sergeant and the perfectly clean sheet of blotting paper in front of him began to get damp. I gave him two and a half minutes of this before question time and then the answers began to slide out easily and with some coherence. What he had to tell me was surprising. In the end he got up, took a bunch of big keys from his pocket, and we went off toward the cell block which at that moment was completely untenanted by criminals.

I suggested that it might be best to let me go alone but the sergeant was now restored to the point where he could face the worst with a certain calm. He unlocked one set of barred doors and then another, switching on lights to mark our progress. The last light brought a bellow which was unmistakably Manson.

By the time we got to him the Bintan Chief of Police was clinging to bars in a manner we've all seen a hundred times in films involving prison procedure. He must have been asleep in the dark, exhausted from an earlier shouting, and there was still a croak in his voice. The sight of the sergeant produced a near-maniacal reaction surprising from a man of his years and experience. His language was bubbling vitriol, both in English and Malay. I had to be stern.

"Manson, I'm not letting you out of there until you calm down."

"What? Calm down! Me?"

"Listen, man, your rugged boy here was trying to do you a good turn. Get that through your head."

"My head! A conk on it with a revolver butt. I've got a lump like an egg on it now. Do you know I was out cold for an hour? He could have killed me!"

"You were scheduled to die another way."

"Is that what he says?"

"I believe him. Your prize trainee hasn't turned out to be one of Yin's quislings. He was on your side all the time. Will you just take a minute off to let that sink in and see what it means?"

The chief did, holding onto the bars. After a time, and some staring at his sergeant, he seemed less like an aging but still dangerously enraged gorilla.

"Your sergeant suspected a lot but couldn't prove anything. All he knew was that he had been tested for loyalty himself and expected that the rest of the force had been tested the same way. And his estimate was just about yours; half had gone over to Yin. But he could never be certain who they were, though he tried. He never had any solid evidence to put to you and was afraid your pride in your force wouldn't let you listen to suspicions. All the man could do was stick by you. That's why you could never shake him off. I think he's been a good boy."

My sermon had a sedative effect. I used the key and the three of us walked out of the detention area into the admin section. Manson, sitting in his own chair, with a big whisky the police only keep for visitors, began to look more like himself. The sergeant had picked up his gun and gone out into the hall.

"What's he doing out there?" Manson asked.

"Looking for other policemen to shoot on sight."

"Eh?"

"When he'd dealt with you he cleared this building, sent everyone home. Said he'd shoot the first man who tried to get in. Not a very comprehensive approach to the local emergency, but I think it probably saved you for your pension. So be grateful. You couldn't have done a damn thing anyway, and you know it. But you can get busy now. You've got one boy who was certainly loyal and probably about twenty more. That's enough police to keep going in a state that's been purged overnight of its really menacing criminal elements."

Manson was in a remarkably comfortable position for his declining years as a career man and he began to see this. Practically every threat to a local policeman's peace of mind was at this moment either wallowing in the jungle trying to get to the Sarawak border or, if he was a big fish like Yin, working his way down the coast to a hoped for and eventual rendezvous with a Chinese junk. Their zeal to get out of the country would be whipped up again every time it flagged by the thought of a princess in control who had sent out a call for pickled heads for her trophy room. Bintan town beneath us practically shone under the stars with a purged purity that mightn't be lasting, but was fine raw material for Manson's second start.

I suggested to him that the thing he wanted to avoid at all costs was Kang's friendly assistance during a time of upheaval and the chief saw my point at once. A few minutes later, hearing an almost bland voice on the phone to Singapore, I knew that the local police crisis was over. I couldn't hear what Kang was saying back, but I guessed he was a disappointed man.

Manson then had the sergeant in for an almost moving reconciliation scene in which the faithful assistant wasn't exactly thanked for what he had done, but near enough. The sergeant was afterward dispatched on a roundup of all policemen who hadn't joined the evacuees, these to be brought in for a quick security screening and almost certain reinstatement in office. After all this had been accomplished the chief, with his own house in order, would be ready for a formal approach to the new Regent to take the oath of allegiance or whatever patter is laid on in a sultanate. I could see that he was just a shade apprehensive about serving under Linau and he admitted being certain for a long time that everything she had been up to was shady. I pointed out that an approach to primitive patriotism often is.

"She had kind words to say about you to the British colonel."

"Really?" Manson seemed surprised.

"The one thing someone up top, no matter how they get there themselves, really appreciates is a public servant who can't be bought, bribed or cajoled. You qualify. If you ask me you're right in, and if you confirm this quickly before the new Resident arrives you ought to have a lot more say in how Bintan is run than he'll ever manage."

"You've a point there, Harris," said the old Far Eastern hand. "Have some more whisky?"

"What I'd really like is a bed for a few hours. One of your cells would do me nicely. Only let me out when I yell, will you?"

TWELVE

URSULA and I walked on her lawn. It hadn't been mown for about a week and now had a shockingly un-English shabbiness, with blue tropic sword grass standing up in insolence. She had asked me back for a cup of tea after the funeral, something not easy to decline, but it had been painful, very unlike the baked-meats ritual I remembered from Scottish relations, where the chief women mourners are totally—and very sensibly—anesthetized to grief by the need to do a vast cooking for a crowd of relations.

Ursula hadn't been obliged to do anything except start to work on making Charlie's ghost acceptable to live with. The phase of self-flagellation with blunt truth was quite over, and she was now back into the normal human pattern of pulling down screen after screen of color-processed falsehood behind which her husband would become a faded but tinted image.

"Look at the way that running weed is taking over," she said. "I must get the garden boy onto it." Then there was an almost startled pause, as though this mundane intrusion into a process of mental embalming was slightly shocking. Her tone changed. "Charles was very fond of you, Paul."

It wasn't something I had ever felt myself and as though she sensed this Ursula strengthened the argument.

"I remember him saying so after your last visit here. How he had enjoyed meeting you. He thought you had an alert mind."

Neither Charlie nor his true ghost could have thought anything of the kind. But I was suddenly conscious of a terrible urgency on Ursula's part over her image-building, as though she had to get something established very quickly indeed, solid enough to cover her suspicions of the truth. Without having the slightest evidence to substantiate this I was certain that she did have these suspicions, and her hurriedly achieved immunity from the real Charlie was feigned. She had been very close to the little man in her way, if not quite his Lady Macbeth, pushing him toward impossible heights for his caliber, her own personality concentrated into a prod for his feeble spirit. It had been an impossible marriage for both in that in it neither could achieve any peace, with a death the only practical solution. Elementary kindness demanded that I assist the survivor.

I said some things about the selflessness demanded of the true colonial servant and these were received with marked enthusiasm. We reached a bed of alien transplants, roses looking anemic in half shade, blown with the heat, pale and scentless. Ursula bent down, aching to get to work on the thorny stems with secateurs, wanting to be busy at an old game of nurturing unhealthy life with continual attention.

"Have you made any plans?" I asked.

She straightened, then turned slowly, looking at her piece of England without looking at me.

"I've decided to stay on here. I got up this morning with the feeling that I must. That Charles would want it."

"I see."

"Don't you approve, Paul?"

The friend of the family status had been clamped down on me.

"We bought this house," she said. "I have a sister in Margate, but England these days is . . . so different, I think this is my world, really. I have my Dyaks and my garden."

I didn't say that there are more durable-seeming worlds for our time and there was a fair chance that Bintan, under

Linau, would outlast Ursula's. Anywhere else she would have a sense of exile, and her thinned blood would feel the cold in Europe.

"My sister lives in a hotel now. I'd hate that. They were in India. Her husband was in the Indian Civil. He got his Knighthood, of course. They lived in Kent when he retired, a lovely place, but Helen simply couldn't get servants and when Henry died the whole thing was impossible. I've been wondering if I mightn't ask her to come out here for a time. Perhaps even for good. Helen is much older than I am, but we always got on very well."

Ursula was going to be all right. She might even manage to be happy when everything was fixed and settled and Charlie's ghost only came back smiling. After all, he'd earned her pension.

In Bintan town it was business as usual. I walked along the main street, past Mr. Chikamongerjee's base shop which gave no hint of the panics of yesterday. I didn't see the proprietor himself, just a Tamil youth who might be one of the large family, busy setting out in pavement trays today's novelty bargains complete with price tags indicating slashing reductions to clear stock. The owners of the big emporium farther along must have felt themselves pure enough to survive any purge of remaining Chinese residents, for there were hints that the place was about to reopen, the boarding coming down. Mixing with the shoppers were a number of paratroopers who didn't look too displeased that their war had been called off, though the town didn't suggest a place taken over by the military. I was sure that the colonel would have most of his men out on mopping-up operations which were certain to mean long sticky hours in the jungle, these unlikely to yield much of a bag in fleeing Reds.

I turned into Wong Kee's garden restaurant to find this also functioning normally, the fountain playing and a third of the stone tables occupied, but no sign of Lil at one of them. A plump Chinese girl in what looked like flowered pajamas, and wearing carpet slippers, waddled over to me with a smiling innocence that could only be deeply rooted in a clear conscience.

"Please seat. What you wanchee I get."

She would, too.

"Do you know Miss Harpen? Have you seen her?"

"Sure. She go post office. She say come back here. You wait? You like coffee, tea, iced dlink?"

"I'll walk on."

"Sure. Come eat Wong Kee's later."

It wasn't in my plans.

The first Resident of Bintan was still standing up outside a Victorian building gazing out toward the future with bronze confidence. I went under the tag to good communications which had been so brilliantly vindicated to find the two young men as unprepared for any work as usual. They looked at me, unhappy about being disturbed, but relieved when it became apparent they weren't going to be.

Lil was inside Bintan's phone box. If she saw me she gave no sign. One of her hands, closed into a fist, was on a shelf, and the girl was staring at her own face in the little mirror provided. Her contact seemed to be doing most of the talking. I sat down on a bench to wait.

This went on for so long that I knew Lil had reversed the charges. Her fist moved sometimes, but the rest of her body was oddly motionless, and she looked coffined away by glass walls into one of the little deaths that are waiting for all of us around corners. I was staring at the floor when the booth door banged.

Lil was standing there wearing a dress, which somehow made her like a stranger, a pale green cotton sheath not really flattering to still-remaining excess fat of adolescence. She had on white shoes and I saw she was wearing one white glove, the other forgotten.

"Oh," she said to me.

"I just came along. It's getting near boat time."

"Yes."

"Going this afternoon hasn't rushed things for you?"

"No. Paul, you know who I was phoning, don't you?"

"I can guess."

"I couldn't find a damn phone anywhere else. They just let me into the Residency to get my things. Thousands of soldiers. I had an escort to my room. It was a laugh."

"I hope you brought everything you'll want?"

"I don't want much."

I thought of the shelves in a room which had been her real base even when she was living on the other side of the world, crowded shelves.

"Did you say goodbye to Linau?"

"Yes. I could only see her for about a minute."

"She'll be busy."

"Not half," Lil said, and laughed.

She didn't make any move toward the doors. Her head came up and her eyes met mine.

"Boots is going to Rome. On the night plane. He couldn't wait."

"Oh."

"They have a three-spot booking in Italy. The rest of the boys are meeting him there. He knew I'd understand. I guess I didn't sound too understanding. The bastard."

She began to cry. I don't know whether I moved or Lil did, but she used my shoulder, a big girl suddenly hanging on, shaking me.

"I'm to . . . to come on to Rome if . . . if I want to. Oh, Paul!"

"It's all right, Lil."

[213]

"It's not all right. It's hell. That little . . . punk."

We had come to the same verdict by different routes.

"If only daddy . . ."

"It'll be all right."

"No it won't. Ever."

She stood back suddenly, still unconscious of the staring clerks.

"What's happened to me?"

"What happens to all of us," I said.

The boat between Bintan and Latuan was a coal burner serving an oil-producing area, an antique built sometime before World War I that had been pushed further and further from civilization as more and more people decided they didn't need it. It had a forward saloon which might have excited Sir Stamford Raffles, the founder of Singapore, but now seemed scarcely worth the extra money to get among all that moldering velours.

Lil and I sat out on deck forward of the funnel where the smuts only got you in a fluke wind, surrounded by our luggage which didn't amount to much for either of us. We sat side by side watching the preparations for the first civilian departure for the outside world since the Regency. There had, of course, been considerable other coming and going, and two slick little corvettes were at anchor, having a brief rest from shooting up and down the coast junk-hunting. I had no information but it would have surprised me to learn that they'd got a prize. The junks would come later for key personnel, if Linau hadn't nabbed these characters first. I knew she'd be trying, but something told me that Yin would in due course be able to walk into that Swiss bank with a golden number which opened the door to life on the Riviera while you rested, and thought again.

"Paul, is there a good secretarial school in Kuala Lumpur?"

"I should think so. Why?"

"I might go to it."

"What about drama college in London?"

"No!"

"You think you'd like to stay out East?"

"Yes. Linau's going to need a good secretary. I might get the job."

We both sat with this thought, watching a sweating Dyak trying to urge a gray water buffalo up two planks onto the ship's lower deck. I couldn't imagine why anyone in Latuan would want a Bintanese water buffalo when they had plenty of their own, but that wasn't my problem. Mine was getting a housekeeper, some capable woman who would make my place on a hill all right for a young ward to live in. I've never had a housekeeper and never wanted one, but I can still see my plain duty when it's shoved at me. Besides, I was beginning to get an odd feeling, not paternal, not even avuncular, just interested. I've never had a hand at an attempt to produce a human being and it was a moderately tempting proposition.

"All right, go to secretarial college."

"You won't mind?"

"I'll like it," I said, before I was sure.

There are certainly duller jobs waiting for a graduate of typing school than being the secretary to a Regent. And it would be keeping the family connection with Bintan.

"How long does it take?" Lil asked. "The course, I mean?"

"If you're bright, six months."

"I'm bright."

She saw Clem first.

"Look who's here."

He came down the deck to us, slouching slightly, back in his role as vacationing newsman with a camera. He even used a tourist's slightly tired smile.

"Greetings, all. Glad I got here in time."

"Is this a bon voyage party? Or are you traveling?"

He shook his head.

"I'm staying. To round out my two weeks. I've been offered a house."

I looked at him.

"Linau's?"

"That's right. She's caught five of her servants already. These ones weren't disloyal, just nervous, and didn't go far. It's pretty awful for her to have to ask me to rub along with only five servants but I told her that after the rest house I didn't mind roughing it."

"You have the house, she has the palace, is that it?"

"Naturally."

"Keep it that way," I said.

"Paul, are you giving me advice?"

"In front of the girl, too. What did you want to see me about?"

"Just wanted to see you. To say goodbye. For now."

"What do you mean, for now?"

"Well, we'll be meeting up again. One of these days. I might run down to Malaya. Or you might care to come up to Hong Kong. Nice sort of neutral ground for both of us. It's been a lovely relationship and I'd hate to see it fade away. Well, all the best to you two."

We watched him stroll off. They had got the water buffalo on board and it was bellowing. Chickens were the last item of cargo.

"Do you want to see Clem again?" Lil asked.

"No," I said. "I don't think I do."

But I knew I was going to. It gave me that cold feeling.

THE PERENNIAL LIBRARY MYSTERY SERIES

Nicholas Blake

THE WORM OF DEATH
THE WHISPER IN THE GLOOM
HEAD OF A TRAVELER
MINUTE FOR MURDER
THE CORPSE IN THE SNOWMAN
THOU SHELL OF DEATH
THE WIDOW'S CRUISE
END OF CHAPTER
THE SMILER WITH THE KNIFE
THE BEAST MUST DIE

Michael Gilbert

DEATH HAS DEEP ROOTS
THE DANGER WITHIN
BLOOD AND JUDGMENT
THE BODY OF A GIRL
FEAR TO TREAD

Andrew Garve

A HERO FOR LEANDA
THE ASHES OF LODA
THE FAR SANDS
NO TEARS FOR HILDA
THE CUCKOO LINE AFFAIR
THE RIDDLE OF SAMSON
MURDER THROUGH THE
LOOKING GLASS

E. C. Bentley

TRENT'S LAST CASE

Cyril Hare

WHEN THE WIND BLOWS
AN ENGLISH MURDER

Julian Symons

THE COLOR OF MURDER
THE 31ST OF FEBRUARY

Gavin Black

YOU WANT TO DIE, JOHNNY?
A DRAGON FOR CHRISTMAS

Arthur Maling

DECOY
DINGDONG